SARAH PURDUE

PAWS FOR LOVE

Complete and Unabridged

LINFORD
Leicester

First published in Great Britain in 2017

First Linford Edition
published 2018

A catalogue record for this book is available
from the British Library.

ISBN 978–1–4448–3908–1

Published by
F. A. Thorpe (Publishing)
Anstey, Leicestershire

Set by Words & Graphics Ltd.
Anstey, Leicestershire
Printed and bound in Great Britain by
T. J. International Ltd., Padstow, Cornwall

This book is printed on acid-free paper

PAWS FOR LOVE

Sam rescues animals and trains assistance dogs — but has less understanding of people! Meanwhile, Henry is desperate to help his young son Toby, who hasn't spoken since his mother died. Toby's therapist has suggested that an assistance dog might help the boy. Unfortunately, Henry Wakefield is terrified of dogs! But when Sam brings Juno into their lives, Toby begins to blossom and Henry starts to relax. Will Juno prove to be a large and hairy Cupid for Sam and Henry?

1

The thick white steam issuing from the bonnet of her elderly motorhome was not a good sign, Sam thought. She was good at turning her hand to most things, but the internal combustion engine remained a little mysterious. With the hazard lights flashing, she told everyone to behave themselves, and popped the bonnet before taking a step back to avoid a steam facial. There was nothing for it, she thought as she grabbed the plastic bottle full of water from the back of the van; it was time for Dotty to go back to the garage.

Sam smiled at all the faces that looked at her from inside Dotty, tails wagging and noses making new imprints on the windows, which she liked to call 'doggy art'. Sam knew enough that she would have to let Dotty cool down before she could top up the radiator, and so she found a spot where she could keep an eye on the kids but stretch her legs out in the early-morning sun.

She heard the sound of a vehicle pulling into the gravel lay-by, and wondered who else was out this early on a Sunday morning. From her vantage point she could see a pair of chinoed legs, with expensive-looking brown loafers, make their way towards her.

'What seems to be the trouble?' the voice associated with those long legs asked her. Sam had to tilt her head right back to look up into the man's face. Even though she was lounging on the grass bank, she realised he was very tall. The sun was travelling up through the sky behind him, so his face was in shadow, and even using her hand to shade her eyes from the light didn't give her a clear view of his features.

'No problem,' she said cheerfully. 'Just Dotty overheating.'

'I'll take a look.' The voice was deep and serious.

'No need,' Sam added, starting to feel annoyed by his attitude, which seemed to assume that she couldn't handle the situation — though she could — and she suspected that this was all about her gender. 'I just need to top up the radiator.'

'Not while the engine's running hot.' The man appeared to be alarmed by her suggestion, as if she couldn't work that one out for herself.

'I know that,' Sam said, a little sharply. What was it with men who felt the need to dive in and rescue you without first checking whether you needed rescuing in the first place? 'Hence the reason why I am taking a moment to enjoy the sun whilst she cools off.'

The man moved now so that the sun was to his left, and Sam could make out the light cotton shirt, one button open at the neck, and skin the colour of a latte, with dark hair that seemed a little too long to go with the rest of his neat and tidy first impression. He looked like a man who was used to being in control.

'Have you got a rag in the van?' he

asked. 'I'll need something to protect my hand when I take the cap off.'

Why did people feel the need to help when you hadn't asked? Sam thought. Life had taught her to be independent, and she wasn't about to give that up to some stranger who seemed to think she was incapable. Without waiting for an answer, the man's long strides took him round to the back of the van, and she heard the catch click as he opened the door. The noise of a rumbling shriek, followed by the kind of language Jean had never let her get away with, made Sam leap to her feet and dash the length of the van. Her mind raced through all the possible things that could have happened to the kids.

But it wasn't the kids. The tall stranger was lying on the ground, and Georgie was giving him her usual welcome, which involved lots of enthusiastic licking and a kind of growling bark which Sam was fairly sure was her version of singing. The rest of the kids were milling around, less interested in the man and more interested in the scents coming off the grassy bank and hedgerow behind. They were well-trained enough to stay out of the road and not wander far.

Her quick visual check told her that the noise hadn't come from any of her dogs, but maybe the man had been so surprised it had escaped before he could control himself. Dog lovers tended to react to her little family with joy, but one look at the man's face told her he was experiencing a quite different emotion. Pure terror was more like it. Georgie, who always assumed everyone loved her as much as she loved them, was now standing with two heavy German Shepherd paws on his chest so that she could get up close and personal and lick his nose.

If the man hadn't looked quite so terrified, Sam probably would have laughed. Instead, she pursed her lips and issued a low whistle. Georgie immediately stopped her loving inspection of the man's face and trotted to sit beside Sam. The rest

of the gang followed suit, in their version of the Von Trapp family, arranged
by size if not by actual age. It was one of
their party tricks that they would show
off at the local charity dog show.

'Stay,' she said softly, before stepping
towards the man. His fear seemed to
have no bounds as he was now
scrabbling backwards away from her on
his elbows. His face was fixed on the
row of dogs and his breathing came
quick and shallow, like he had just run
from a pack of wolves.

'Easy there,' Sam said, holding out
her hand, as she did with all spooked
animals she came across. 'Here, let me
help you up.' She spoke softly, but the
man's eyes snapped to her face.

'There should be a law against it,' he
said, his voice pitched rather higher
than it had been earlier.

Sam raised an eyebrow.

'Against what? Strangers opening the
back door of a person's motorhome
and letting her well-behaved dogs out?'

'Well-behaved?' The man had now

crawled so far that his back was resting on the bonnet of his new Mercedes, and he seemed to find courage in its vicinity. 'They're like a pack of wolves!'

Sam treated him to her thousand-yard stare, one she usually reserved for lowlifes who mistreated animals.

'Georgie was just saying hello. There's nothing to be afraid of.'

That seemed like a red rag to a bull. The man levered himself up off the gravel and started to brush himself down.

'Not everyone loves dogs,' he said gruffly as if that explained his extreme over reaction. 'Dog owners should bear that in mind.'

'We do,' Sam said, trying to ignore the fact that she didn't trust people who didn't love dogs. 'I haven't forced my animals on you. You took it upon yourself that I needed rescuing, and let them out before I could do anything.'

'And that's the thanks I get for offering my assistance.'

Sam crossed her arms over her chest.

7

Behind her, she could feel Georgie creeping forward like a shadow, as she did when she felt something wasn't right and that Sam might need her. Not that anyone who knew Georgie would be worried. She was the soppiest dog Sam had ever met, but her bulk and bark often gave a completely different impression.

'It wasn't exactly an offer, though, was it? I tried to tell you I was fine, but you assumed that I was incapable of helping myself.'

Sam reached a hand down and stroked Georgie's ruff. It was a clear sign to Georgie that everything was fine, and she felt her lean in, just as a reminder that she was there. Sam smiled down at her and then looked back up. The man had backed away and yanked open the car door. He was inside before she could blink. He rolled down the window an inch, clearly worried that one of the small dogs might try and jump inside his precious car, and glared at Sam.

'I will bear that in mind for the future,' he said, his voice making it clear that he felt he was an entirely innocent victim, and with a squeal of tyres he was off.

Sam looked down at Georgie and rolled her eyes. Georgie seemed to completely understand her, even if people didn't.

2

'Right, kids, show's over.' At her hand direction, the dogs jumped back into the van, and Sam slammed the door shut before heading back to the bonnet to refill the radiator.

With Dotty protesting just a little, Sam and the dogs finally made it home. They had to stop once more to let Dotty cool down. Tomorrow Sam was definitely going to have to call the garage.

She was standing in the small shed that had been converted into her office. The kids were all out in the acre of land that used to be a working orchard and still provided plenty of apples for Jimbo and Mac, Sam's two rescue ponies.

Now everyone had been fed and watered, except for her, Sam turned her attention to her work diary. She had a couple of appointments today, and she wasn't sure she would have time to eat. Later, she had Violet, an ex-racing greyhound who had been kept in a shed for most of her young life. Sam had been working with her for several months, building up trust, and it was starting to pay off. It wouldn't be long before Sam could sign her off, and hopefully the charity caring for her would be able to find her a good home.

The first appointment was a new client, a family who were looking for an assistance dog. Sam's work involved all sorts, but aside from the rehabilitation of animals who had been mistreated, finding the right dog for an individual and training them to assist their owner was her favourite, albeit the most time-consuming, part of her job. This was an initial meeting to discuss with the client what they needed the dog to be able to do. She wondered if the new client had a particular breed in mind; that could always be tricky, as for Sam, it was all down to the individual dog's personality, and breed had little to do with it.

Glancing at the clock on the wall, she saw she had maybe five minutes. Just enough time to make a coffee and see if there were any biscuits left in the jar.

With a steaming cup in one hand and a jammy dodger, her favourite, in the other, she walked back into the small office just as she heard the sound of a car pulling up outside. A quick look behind her told her the gate out to the back yard, as she liked to call it, was pulled shut; although she could see various members of her pack racing around whilst Georgie and Bennie, her Miniature Dachshund, sunned themselves on the patio.

Sam lifted the hatch in the counter and walked to open the door. The car had pulled up right in front of the small office, the driver seemingly ignoring the signs which would allow several vehicles to park in the provided spaces. Sam sighed; sometimes people were so focused that they missed the obvious. What they needed to do, she thought, was slow down a bit and follow the example of animals. The car door opened but the person quickly disappeared, opening the back door on the opposite side and ducking down out of sight.

When the tall figure reappeared, he was carrying a small boy in his arms. Sam wasn't great with judging kids' ages, but she guessed he was around four or five, so to her he seemed a little old to be carried. As the man turned to push the car door closed with a free hand, Sam caught a glance of his face — and felt the fizz of excitement that she usually had on meeting new clients burn out.

He was the interfering driver from the lay-by.

Knowing that this was going to be awkward, whatever she did, she decided to get the meet-and-greet over and done with, and started to walk towards the car.

'Mr Wakefield,' Sam said, holding out a hand for him to shake. 'I'm Sam Fletcher. It's good to meet you.' Sam decided to leave off the 'again' part of that comment, since it was clear from the frozen look on his face that he remembered her as well as she remembered him.

'And who is this?' Sam asked, feeling the need to say something. Wakefield just looked at her, and Sam wondered if he was considering shoving his kid back into the car and driving off at speed, as he had done earlier; but her question seemed to prompt him to look at his child, and Sam saw a battle quietly rage.

'This is Toby, my son.'

'Hi Toby,' Sam said, but Toby made no reply, merely stared at her with wide eyes and tightened his grip on his dad's neck. Wakefield, for his part, rubbed his son's back, and Sam wondered if the older man's apparent fear of dogs had been passed on a generation. She frowned, trying to work out what Wakefield could possibly want. She was sure he had said he wanted to discuss an assistance dog on the phone, but she must have misheard him.

Realising that they were all standing as if paralysed in the middle of the small parking area, Sam held out a hand.

'Why don't you come through? We can sit down and talk about what it is I can do for you.'

Again, Sam wondered if he would bolt, but as she watched he took a deep breath, this time with only a slight shudder, and fell into step behind her. Sam directed them to a small seating area with an elderly couch and pulled up her office chair. She followed his gaze to the wooden open-slat gate where Georgie, nosey as ever, had decided to look over.

'The gate is closed, Mr Wakefield.' She tried a reassuring smile, which seemed to have little effect. 'Now,' she said, picking up a clipboard with a client information sheet on it and clicking her pen, 'perhaps you could start by telling me how I can help you today?'

15

She wondered if he had got the wrong idea about her. She was an animal therapist; she dealt with animals. If he had come to her in the hope that she could help him with his obvious fear of dogs, she knew he had come to the wrong place. The only thing she could offer him was total immersion therapy, and she doubted that would help.

'We discussed a bespoke assistance dog on the phone,' Wakefield said, his eyes flicking from the gate to her face and back again. Sam nodded.

'For you?' she asked doubtfully. She couldn't see what he might need assistance with, but knew from experience that some people's disabilities were hidden.

'No!' he said, and let out what could only be described as a strangled laugh, as if a dog would be the last thing on his Christmas list. 'For Toby,' he said, his focus now completely on his son.

Sam allowed him to have that moment; she sensed there was quite a

16

story there, perhaps a difficult one to tell, so she waited. All the man's attention was focused on his son, and he continued to rub the boy's back gently, although now Sam wasn't sure if it was for the boy's comfort or for his own.

'If you can just give me a minute, I will call my assistant, Jean. Perhaps she can play with Toby whilst we talk?' Without waiting for a reply, Sam pulled her mobile phone out of her pocket and sent a quick text.

'I'm not sure . . . ' Wakefield started to say. 'It would be easier to discuss matters . . . but Toby . . . Toby finds it difficult with new people.'

'I understand,' Sam said, with what she hoped was a reassuring smile. 'Jean has worked with children for many years. I like to call her the child whisperer,' she added, hoping to lighten the mood, but Wakefield was too lost in his own world to hear what she was saying.

They were all rescued in that moment as a voice drifted in from the back yard. Jean was saying hello to all the various creatures that greeted her enthusiastically. The half-back-gate opened, and an older woman with long grey hair running free across her shoulders appeared.

'Hello,' Jean said, and somehow they all knew that she was speaking to Toby. He still had his arms wrapped around his dad's neck, but he at least turned his face towards her. Jean moved so that she was much nearer, and then knelt down so that they were on the same level.

'You must be Toby,' Jean said, and the little boy nodded, his eyes wide but fixed on her warm, gentle face. Jean nodded seriously. 'I'm not sure if your dad has told you what we do here, but we help animals.' Toby said nothing, but it was as if Jean expected silence. Sam marvelled once again at her ability to read people and situations.

'Well, I have some work to do with a rabbit and guinea pig, and to be honest I need some help.' Jean's face showed a thoughtful expression. 'The thing is, Sam here — ' She turned and gestured.

' — is kind of busy with your dad, and I really do need someone else who can come and help. Someone who can be gentle and not scare them.'

Sam wasn't sure, but she thought she could see a little light burn in Toby's eyes. Jean was working her magic. She watched as Jean walked to a door, next to a large floor-to-ceiling window on the right side of the office, which led to the small animal therapy room.

'I'm going to get my friends out now. Would you like to come and see them?' Jean was watching Toby's face closely, as was Wakefield. 'You can bring your dad,' she added as she moved into the room.

Sam watched a silent conversation happen between Toby and his father, and Toby slowly climbed out of his embrace, though still gripping his dad's hand tightly, and they walked together into the small room. The room itself had another large window, and so was filled with natural daylight. The floor was covered in carpet that looked like

19

grass, and Jean had started to get out some of the toys that she used in her treatments. Wakefield, it seemed, didn't have any issues with small animals, and so he led his son into the room and together they sat down cross-legged on the carpet.

'Here,' Jean said, handing Toby a soft square of blanket. 'Betsy here gets frightened very easily, and so she likes to just sit on our laps as we stroke her gently. Do you think you could do that?'

Toby nodded solemnly, and carefully arranged the blanket on his lap before Jean gently placed the downy brown rabbit into his arms. Sam watched as the world around Toby seemed to disappear and he was lost in the moment. Jean reached out a hand for Wakefield's arm.

'Toby will be fine here with me, Mr Wakefield. He can see you through the window, and I will bring him straight out to you if he needs you.'

Wakefield looked at Jean as if she

were some kind of miracle worker —
which, of course, Sam knew she was
— and his eyes seemed to glisten with
tears that could flow at any moment.

'Thank you,' he said, his voice soft, as
if he were afraid of breaking the spell
that Toby seemed to be under. 'And it's
Henry, please.'

Jean smiled. 'Very nice to meet you,
Henry. Now go and speak to Sam. Toby
and I will be fine.'

3

Sam handed Henry the cup of coffee she had made, and placed the plate of biscuits on the small table. It was clear to her that he needed it: she suspected that he spent all his energy on his son, and had little left to address his own day-to-day needs. She had turned the sofa so that Henry could sit facing the window and see Toby in the next room.

'So, you would like Toby to have an assistance dog?' Her brain was still struggling to reconcile the fear she had seen earlier when he had met her pack with the man sat in front of her requesting a dog, but she was also in no doubt that his son was his number-one priority.

Henry tore his eyes away from the window, and Sam focused all her attention on him. She didn't need to be told that what he was about to share would be difficult and painful.

'Toby hasn't said a word for nearly two years. Before — before he lost his mum, we could barely keep up with his chattering.'

Sam looked at the small boy, sat cradling the tiny rabbit. He looked as if he had lost his mother that morning, and was in the complete and over-whelming shock of that new reality.

'I've tried everything.' Henry's voice cracked a little, and Sam had no doubt that he was speaking the truth. 'Everything to reach him. We have a new therapist, and he feels that Toby needs to bond with something. Some-thing he can learn to trust, who can maybe even go to school with him. He suggested a dog, and I found you on the web.'

Henry seemed to find the whole conversation exhausting, as if it repre-sented the burden he felt at being unable to reach his son, who had pulled up the drawbridge and withdrawn. The pain in the air was palpable, but Sam felt she needed to say something that Henry might not like.

'Mr Wakefield . . . ' Sam began, wondering how to word her concerns. There was no way an assistance dog could be successful in an environment where the adult of the household was permanently terrified. She admired the man, who was prepared to try and face his worst fears to help his son, but she still needed to consider the welfare of any future canine companion.

'Please, call me Henry,' he said, and ran a hand through his slightly-too-long hair. 'And I know what you're going to say. I know, after earlier, that you . . . ' He didn't seem to be able to find the words to explain what had happened earlier in the day, so Sam just nodded, and he seemed a little relieved. 'My mother and my sister, they've said the same, that it's madness. I can't say it was first on my list of options, but I'm desperate. Toby, he is everything to me, and I have to . . . '

There were other words unspoken,

and when Sam looked into those clear blue eyes she knew that he was asking her for something else. It wasn't just Toby who needed her help — it was him too. This man was so desperate to reach his son, to break him free from the castle of grief he had locked himself in, to help him be a little boy again, that he was prepared to face his worse fear. She knew that he was studying her, and she could also read his expression. His fear of dogs was not the worst thing. The worst thing that could happen to him was his son being locked away from him for the rest of his life.

Sam didn't work with people. In fact, anyone who knew her would likely categorise her as being happier with four-legged — or, in some cases, three-legged — creatures. Animals, she understood; people, not so much. But she had personal experiences of the healing power of dogs, and if ever two people need that — well, they were sat in front of her, and she was going to help them.

'Mr Wakefield . . . '

'Henry, please,' he said, and Sam could tell that he meant it: it was almost a plea. ''Mr Wakefield' makes me feel like I'm my father,' he added with a small frown, as if that were enough of an explanation. Sam nodded thoughtfully, and filed that new piece of information away for later; something she often did when she met traumatised dogs for the first time.

'Henry. Perhaps it would help if I explain the process involved.'

Henry looked up, and Sam could see something like hope on his face.

'All of the dogs I train to be assistance dogs are rescue animals. I find I get the best results from them.'

Henry looked concerned, glancing briefly in the direction of his son, who was sitting on the floor completely immersed in the care of his rabbit.

'If we want to be successful, then it is important that Toby and the dog bond well right from the start.'

Henry nodded, and with an effort

26

forced his gaze away from the small boy to Sam's face.

'I work with a couple of local charities and a few foster homes. I'll visit them and pick out a few dogs I think might be possibilities. Then I'll need Toby to come and meet them.'

Sam watched Henry's reaction carefully; just like dogs when they were stressed, he swallowed and licked his lips. Sam hid a small smile; perhaps people weren't so different, or as difficult to read, as she had imagined. Words seemed to escape him, so he simply nodded his agreement.

'Right. Perhaps you could tell me a little bit more about Toby. Is there anything he is particularly frightened of?'

Henry glanced once again at his son.

'Everything seems to frighten him. Before . . . ' His voice wobbled a little, and it seemed he couldn't say the words out loud. He cleared his throat and carried on. 'Before everything happened, he was carefree, you know?'

Sam nodded, not wanting to speak and break the spell.

'We had trouble keeping up with him. He was fearless, willing to have a go at anything. Needless to say, we had several visits to the Accident & Emergency department.' He smiled, lost in a memory of the past. 'But now, he won't let me out of his sight.' Henry frowned as he realised that Toby had recently managed to do just that, and he turned once again to gaze at his son. 'I have to work, and my mum and sister help out, but he's missing out on so much. We can barely get him to school, and most of the time they call to have us come and collect him within the first hour. It's a severe form of separation anxiety; not really a surprise, considering, but it should have eased by now. If anything, it's getting worse.'

Henry leaned back into the sofa, and it looked like all the air had been sucked out of him, as if the weight of repeating the story had deflated him. Sam could see how tired he was, and so she let him have this moment. She turned to look at Toby, and watched as he gently stroked a guinea pig before offering it a lettuce leaf.

Sam had seen the healing power of a dog many times before. She had seen how they had transformed lives. Toby's situation was desperate, but the right dog would surely only help him heal. Whatever it took, she was going to help him. It would be a challenge, especially since Henry had such an obvious fear, but maybe the right dog could help with that too.

'So, as I said, the first step is finding some candidates that I think would work for Toby,' She didn't add the 'and you' part, but it would definitely have to be a factor. 'I'll visit some of the shelters tomorrow and let you know if I find some suitable dogs to introduce Toby to. This part can take a few weeks, but it's important that we find a good match.'

Henry nodded, opened his mouth to speak, and then closed it again.

'Once I have a few in mind, I'll give you a call so we can arrange for Toby to meet them. It should be fairly obvious to both of us if he finds the right companion.'

'Thank you,' Henry said, standing up and holding out his hand. Sam returned the gesture.

'It may take time, but I'm sure we can help Toby,' she added, knowing that it would be the dog who worked all the magic.

Without another word, they both moved to look through the window. Jean was close by, keeping an eye on Toby but letting him be. Toby seemed lost in the moment: it was the first time Sam had seen him without an expression of total fear on his face.

'I haven't seen him like this for so long,' Henry said, giving voice to Sam's thoughts. 'It's like getting a glimmer of the real Toby that's trapped inside.' The emotion in Henry's voice was so strong that Sam overcame her usual reluctance for physical contact with people, and reached out for his hand to give it a brief squeeze. Henry looked down at her, and he seemed as surprised as she was by the move. Sam looked away, not wanting to give the wrong impression, but when she looked back Henry was still staring at her. She smiled to hide her embarrassment.

'Well, I'd best be getting on,' Sam said; which was a lie since Violet, her next patient, wasn't going to arrive until the afternoon, 'You and Toby can stay for as long as you like. I have your number so I'll give you a call.' Realising that she was starting to babble, she turned on her heel and headed out into the back yard.

4

Sam sat in the waiting room of Muddy Paws Rescue and waited. She had managed to find three dogs which she thought would be suitable companions for Toby, but it all now rested on that magic that she couldn't control. Most dogs loved people, but she was looking for more than that. With Toby, it would need to be an instant connection, and Sam couldn't help but worry. She shook her head and pushed the thought from her mind. If none of these three was the one, then she would just keep looking.

The real problem, she knew — but would never say out loud — was that she wasn't sure she could bear the disappointment from Henry. He had been arrogant and condescending in their first meeting, but since then she had seen a whole different side to him.

A man who was desperate to reach his son. Sam's own family life had been messy and painful, but she saw in Henry a man who really was a dad. And Sam wanted to help him, not to mention Toby.

From her seat, she could see the entrance to the small car park, and had to resist the urge to jump up every time she heard a car approach. The receptionist, Kay, was giving her funny looks, and Sam did her best to look as if she hadn't noticed.

A red Fiesta pulled into the lot, and an elderly woman climbed out before opening the boot and pulling out a set of dog stairs. A large hound of indeterminate breed, but with the bearing of an elderly statesman, walked down the stairs. He gave his owner an imperious look — Sam wondered if her driving skills had been below par — and then they walked together through the open door to the reception area.

'Mrs Grays-Bowles and Colonel

Bowles. Lovely to see you again. I'll let Melissa know you are here. Archie is very excited to be going home with you.'

Sam watched as the white-haired lady and her pooch exchanged dignified looks. 'If you mean Archibald, then yes, dear. The Colonel and I are delighted that he can finally come home with us.' She smiled benevolently at Kay, who opened a door which led them through to the back.

There was the sound of another car, and this time, without worrying about what Kay might think, Sam did actually bounce up out of her chair. Henry's Mercedes looked distinctly out of place surrounded by the other cars, which were not quite old enough to be considered 'classic', but did look like they needed intensive restoration. Dotty was parked up near the back, but today Sam had left all the kids at home.

Henry appeared, with Toby once again in his arms. He looked pale and as if he was having trouble taking a deep breath. His fear was no less obvious than if he had the word tattooed across his forehead.

'Ah, now I get it,' Kay said, her voice sounding close behind Sam, making her jump since she hadn't heard the receptionist return. Sam wanted to deny whatever Kay was accusing her of, but Henry was surely now within hearing distance, and she knew that it wouldn't help the situation.

'Henry, Toby, good to see you,' Sam said, plastering a smile on her face, hoping that it might go some way to reduce the tension. Henry didn't smile, just swallowed; and, since he looked like he might collapse at any moment, Sam led them both to the waiting-room chairs. Henry sank down into one with a flash of what might have been gratitude.

'So, Toby, has your dad told you what we're going to do today?'

Toby's eyes were as wide as his father's, but he at last managed to nod his head.

'I have three different dogs I want you to meet. It's really important for you and your new dog to get along, so you need to tell me what you think.'

Toby nodded again, but then turned his face into his dad's chest.

'I was thinking, Toby, that maybe you and I could go and meet these dogs, and leave your dad here?'

Toby didn't need to speak to give his reply; even Sam could see his small body start to shake and his grip round his dad's neck tighten. Sam wished she had Jean with her. Jean always knew how to handle people, and children in particular; she just always seemed to know what to do and what to say.

'Okay, Toby, no problem. Your dad can come with us.'

Henry nodded with what looked like a supreme effort. Sam wanted to reach out and reassure him again, but after his last reaction, not to mention all the thoughts that had flown through her own head, she had promised herself to keep a professional distance. This was about Toby, after all.

'Right, well, we are going to go through that door over there into one of the introduction rooms.' She said the words slowly, as much for Henry's benefit as Toby's. 'It's a bit like the therapy room back at my place. Then one of the volunteers will bring the first dog in to meet you. We'll have some toys, and we can just have a play and see how you feel.'

Sam stood up and waited for Henry to join her. Everything about him told her that he wanted to be anywhere but where he was, so Sam stayed still, giving him time, just as she would when meeting a terrified animal. Henry gave Toby a squeeze, then lifted his head and set his jaw. Sam took that as a sign that she should lead the way.

They walked through the door and down a corridor. Through the first window, Mrs Grays-Bowles and Colonel Bowles could be seen greeting Archibald, a sausage dog with an impossibly long body and short legs.

Sam smiled: she loved seeing families created. She only hoped she would have the same success with Toby and Henry.

Sam pushed open the next door and held it open so that Henry and Toby could walk through. Henry scanned the room, and Sam wondered if he were checking for escape routes.

'Shall we sit on the floor?' Sam said, directing her comment at Toby; but the boy wasn't ready to let go of his dad, so Henry pulled him into his lap and sat on the sofa.

There was a gentle knock on the door.

'Toby, I'd like you to meet Roxy.' Sam took the lead from the young volunteer and gave her a smile. Roxy was the smallest dog Sam had been able to find that she thought might work for Toby. She was a mixture of Jack Russell and Chihuahua.

'Roxy is three years old, Toby, so a little younger than you.'

Toby nodded, but didn't move from his spot. Roxy was sniffing around the floor but not paying Toby much heed.

'Do you want to stroke her?' Henry said to Toby. 'Maybe we should sit on the floor like Sam? She can't really see you up here.' Henry's voice sounded encouraging, and so Sam thought that maybe he would be able to cope with Roxy. Henry shifted as if he was going to sit on the floor, but Toby shook his head and hid his face.

'Okay,' Sam said, knowing she had seen enough. 'I think I'll take Roxy back and pick up Milo.'

Henry's face creased in a frown. He had obviously had high hopes for Roxy, and maybe he was worried, like Sam was, that Toby wasn't ready to make a bond with a dog.

Milo bounded into the room, and Sam was glad that she had a tight hold of his lead. He made a beeline for Henry, who sat as still as a statue, and Sam thought she could see him shake just a little. Milo was making a high-pitched yipping noise and trying to scrabble up onto the sofa. One look at Toby's face told Sam that Milo was not for him.

Standing outside the door again, Sam took in a deep breath, addressing the final candidate. 'Right, boy, this is important. I know that you want a new home; but that little boy in there, he needs a friend, and I think you might be the one. So, let's put our best paw forward.'

Juno seemed to have understood every word as he walked slowly into the room beside her and then sat obediently as Sam closed the door. Sam decided that it was time for an all-or-nothing approach, and so she unclipped the lead from the dog's collar. Juno glanced up at her, and then walked over to the sofa before resting his head in Toby's lap. Sam held her breath as Toby's eyes went wide, and she wondered if he was going to start screaming. Juno shifted a little and whined, and Toby held out a hand and tentatively scratched his ears.

Sam felt overwhelmed with relief,

reaching out for the plastic chair and sitting down. She had been so frightened that she wouldn't find Toby the right match, and here he was, gently stroking Juno with the ghost of a smile on his face. Sam could feel hotness behind her eyes and blinked; it wasn't her place to cry over Toby's reaction, that was for Henry.

She sought out his face and didn't see what she expected. He didn't look happy. He didn't even look frightened. He simply looked furious.

5

Sam stared, wondering if she was misreading his expression. He looked so angry, as if Sam had done something terrible, when in fact all she had done was perform a miracle with the help of her canine friend.

'Toby seems to have made his choice,' Sam said hopefully, wondering if it was just the shock. Perhaps it was only now that Henry was dealing with the reality of having to take a dog home with him.

'Can I talk to you outside for a minute, please?'

Toby looked up at his dad's sharp words and the ghost of a smile was gone, replaced by the familiar fear. Henry bent down.

'I'll be right out there. I'll stand by the window so you can see me all the time,' Henry said, his voice soft.

Toby shook his head, just as Juno leaned into him. Toby screwed up his face as Juno licked him on the nose. Toby looked at Juno and then to his dad and nodded solemnly. Henry stood up, his eyes fixed on his son, and somehow managed to navigate his way to the door. He closed the door and stood so that he could see Toby and Toby could see him.

Sam still couldn't work out what was going on. Surely this had been what Henry had wanted? Sam's eyes flicked from Toby — who had his arms around Juno's neck — to Henry's face, which looked stonily back at her.

'Did you do that on purpose?' he snapped, and Sam took a step back.

'If you mean *find your son the right dog*, then yes, I did.' She knew she was pushing back when she should put on her professional hat, but where did this guy get off? His child had just nearly smiled for possibly the first time in years.

'And I supposed it had to be the

43

biggest, hairiest dog you could possibly find?' He gestured through the window at the large yellow animal. 'It's not a dog — it's more like a small pony!'

'In which case it shouldn't bother you,' Sam said, her tone moving to icy.

Henry was shaking his head and staring at Juno.

'Maybe you should stop focusing on Juno and look at your son.'

Henry's brow furrowed, but he did look at Toby, and it was as if he was seeing him for the first time.

'I told you that it is important that it's a good match. I didn't pick Juno; Toby did.' She watched as Juno nudged at Toby, who had stopped stroking him to look up, his eyes seeking his dad.

Henry waved and managed a smile. Toby waved back, but his eyes suggested he would be happier with his dad back in the room. When Henry looked back at Sam, there was no trace of the smile; instead, he looked suspicious. Sam rolled her eyes. Did he really think she would pick a dog just because of his size to annoy him? He clearly didn't know her very well. All Sam wanted was for Henry to go away. She felt like he had marred one of the special moments in her life, and for that she wouldn't care if she never saw him again. She would have to, of course, for Toby's sake and for Juno's. They all needed this to work.

'I'll take Juno back to my place with me,' Sam said, deciding that professional was the way to go. 'I'll need you to bring Toby in every day. What time is good for you?'

Henry looked surprised at the change in tone, but didn't comment on it. 'Perhaps straight from school?' Sam watched as he did a quick calculation in his head. 'Around four?'

'That will be fine. I'll work on basic obedience commands first. Then we can look to what we need Juno to do if Toby is anxious or upset.'

Henry nodded, his gaze back on his son, who continued to hug the large dog. He turned back to Sam and opened his mouth to speak, but Sam didn't want to hear any more, so she dashed back into the room to cut him off.

'Well, Toby,' she said, crouching down besides the dog and the small boy, 'I think you and Juno make a great pair.' The boy looked up at her, and he seemed less afraid than he had previously, with one arm hanging around the dog's middle.

'I'm going to take Juno home with me so I can train him to do everything you need him to do.'

Toby was shaking his head and frowning.

'It's okay, buddy. We're going to visit Juno every day.' Henry was back in full parent mode, and Sam was more than a little relieved. Small children were sometimes the most difficult parts of the human race for her to figure out.

'Sam is going to train him so that he sits when you tell him to. It's a bit like doggy school. He has to go to school just like you do.'

Toby remained stubbornly unconvinced, and in fact looked rather sorry
for his furry companion.

'The harder we work, Toby, the
sooner Juno can come home and live
with you,' Sam added.

Toby turned to his dad with a
quizzical look. Sam bit back a smile.

'Yes,' Henry reassured him, 'if we can
get him to do everything we need him
to, he can come and live with us.'

Toby arched a suspicious eyebrow.

'I promise, bud,' Henry said, laughing. He smiled at his son and then
smiled up at Sam. Sam hadn't been
expecting to be included in the family
amusement, so her face was worryingly
dour-looking, and she watched as the
smile on Henry's face slipped a little.
He turned his attention back to Toby,
and Sam sighed inwardly. This was the
problem with people, she decided.
Animals seemed to be able to see
through you and know what you really
felt. They never made you feel like you
were getting it wrong, like people did.

Sam's desire to get out of that room and home to her animals was strong, but she knew she had to try and remain professional.

'Right,' she said, picking up the lead and clipping it to Juno's collar. She gave him a friendly pat on the head. 'I have some paperwork to fill out, but Toby, I will see you tomorrow after school.' She tried out a smile on the boy and he nodded, keeping his eyes fixed on Juno.

Sam desperately wanted to walk out of the room, but she wasn't sure how Toby would react to seeing his dog disappear. With effort, she looked to Henry for some guidance. Henry nodded as if he understood the unspoken question.

'Give him a hug, Toby,' Henry said, and pulled out his mobile phone to take a photograph. 'Look, I'll print this out on the computer for you when we get in.' Henry waggled the phone in Toby's direction, and Toby let go of Juno long enough to take in the picture. 'Straight from school tomorrow, I promise,' Henry said. Toby nodded, and moved so that he was standing solemnly by his dad.

Henry headed to the door and Toby followed in his wake, dragging his feet. When they reached the door, Toby turned ran back to Juno, threw his arms around Juno's neck, and let the dog lick his nose once more. With a scrunched-up face and an almost-smile, Toby followed his dad back out towards the reception are.

Sam felt for the sofa behind her and sat down. People, she thought, looking at Juno who sat there and appeared for all the world as if he was smiling, were exhausting.

'Right then, boy. You're going to come home with me. We need to make sure your behaviour is exemplary. I don't think Henry there is going to cope with anything less.' Juno looked up at her, tongue lolling out, panting a little.

'But Toby, the little boy? He's the one you need to work your magic on.'

Juno let out a short bark, and Sam knew that he understood.

6

Sam and Juno were practising sitting on command in the back yard, with the rest of the gang looking on. Georgie was lolling on the patio area, having got bored several sits ago. A few of the other members of her pack didn't seem to be able to help themselves, and also stood and sat on command. It made her smile, but she forced herself to focus on Juno. He needed to get this right, and he did just fine as long as there were no distractions.

There was movement to Sam's left and at the edge of her eyeline. She knew it was a squirrel. She glanced back at Juno and willed him to ignore it. But Juno was having none of it; his eyes went wide and then he became a yellow blur, a giant yellow blur.

'Juno!' Sam called, although she knew it was no use. The squirrel, used to being chased, was in no real danger. He made it with ease to an apple tree and scampered up the trunk, leaving Juno barking and whining at the bottom.

'Sam? Henry and Toby are here,' Jean called from the direction of the office, and Sam winced. Juno was not making a great second impression, paws halfway up the tree's trunk and barking like a thing possessed. Fixing a smile on her face, she turned around to greet them. Henry was clearly not happy to come out into the yard with all the 'highly dangerous' dogs, and had one arm round Toby, restraining him behind the half-gate. She waved, and Toby gave a little wave in return.

'Juno!' she called hopefully. They hadn't worked on recall yet, and so it was no real surprise that it had no effect. Juno continued to bark, the pitch going up an octave. With her back to him, Sam couldn't see Henry, but she knew he was glaring at her. Juno was probably displaying all the worst dog traits in Henry's mind.

Sam set her shoulders back and walked across the old orchard to Juno's side. He looked at her with one eye, keeping his other eye fixed on the squirrel, who was darting around the top branches performing the squirrel equivalent of poking his tongue out.

'Juno, this is important.'

Juno blinked.

'Okay, I know the squirrel is also important; but Toby is here, and he . . . ' Sam didn't get any further. It was if she had fired a starter gun and Juno was in a race. He bounded across the orchard in long, gangly strides. When he reached the half-back-gate that kept the kids out of the office, he looked like he was going to jump for it. Sam could see Henry start to backpedal away from the gate, dragging Toby along with him.

By the time Sam got to the gate, breathless and red in the face, Juno had vaulted it and was doing a little dance around Toby. Henry had Toby in his arms, lifting him out of Juno's reach; whilst all the while Toby was trying to get to his dog. It was a recipe for disaster.

'Perhaps if you put Toby down, Juno will calm down?' Jean suggested, and reached out a steady hand for Henry's arm. But Henry was lost in the fear of the moment, and all he could do was continue to try and back away.

'Juno, sit!' Sam bellowed above the noise of Juno's frustrated barking. She squeezed her eyes closed for a split second, not sure that she could bear to see Juno ignore the command. But Juno was a smart cookie: he obviously realised that this was a good time to obey, and he sat and whined for Toby. Sam moved to press a comforting hand on Juno's head. She risked a quick glance in Jean's direction, but Jean looked as calm as always.

'Henry, I really do think it would be okay to put Toby down,' Sam said.

Henry remained standing with Toby locked in his embrace.

'Juno's calm now,' Sam said. 'It's a good sign that he reacted so strongly to Toby's presence. It means they have formed a strong bond already ... ' Sam's voice trailed away as she saw Henry glare at her. Sam looked to Jean again for guidance.

'How about I put the kettle on? Henry, you look like you could do with a drink,' Jean said.

Sam thought Henry could probably do with something much stronger than the tea that Jean would make, but kept that thought to herself, particularly as it was followed with the idea that maybe Henry could get some of those herbal calming tablets from the chemist. She was pretty sure Henry would not appreciate the suggestion.

Henry leaned down so that Toby could put his feet on the floor, but it was only when Toby tugged at his arms that he let the boy go. Toby seemed a little shy and took a step towards Juno, uncertainly. Juno looked up at Sam, and she gave him a nod; hoping that he understood that now was the time for calm, however excited he was.

There was silence save for the click of Juno's claws on the tiled floor. He walked slowly over to Toby and sat down. Toby reached out a hand, and Juno lifted his head up higher so that it was almost like Juno was stroking Toby's hand, not the other way round. Toby got to his knees and threw his arms around Juno, who yipped with happiness.

Henry looked as if he was about to fall over. Jean had reappeared with a tray of tea and some biscuits. With her head, she gestured to Sam that she should get Henry to sit down. Sam held out her hand, but all of Henry's attention was on the dog. It seemed as if he thought something bad would happen if he looked away.

Sam reached out a hand and tugged him on the arm, back a few steps, until he could feel the sofa behind him. He sank into it with the suggestion that his knees had given up.

'Here,' Jean said, sitting down on the office chair and handing Henry a mug. 'I don't know if you take sugar, but I've put some in. You look like you need it.'

Sam smiled, Jean always said things in such a way that left little room for argument.

When Henry had sipped some of the hot, sweet tea, and a little of the tension had gone from his shoulders, Sam decided it was safe to speak.

'Juno is doing well . . . ' she started. Henry turned his watchful eyes from his son to glare at Sam. But she had been expecting this reaction, and had schooled her face not to react.

'Really, he is. It's only been twenty-four hours, and he has mastered the 'sit' command.' In her head, she added 'as long as there are no squirrels around'. Sam could feel Jean's cool gaze, and flashed her a small guilty smile.

'That's great,' said Henry, his voice giving the impression that he thought it was anything but. 'However, since Toby can't currently speak, I would still say we have a pretty big problem.'

Now Sam smiled broadly. She had already anticipated this, which was why she had trained Juno to respond to the hand signals she used with deaf dogs. She stood up and moved to crouch down besides Toby.

'Right, Toby, we need to start practising some commands with Juno.'

Toby nodded, but looked worried.

'So, we are going to start with the command to get Juno to sit. Stand beside me,' Sam said, getting to her feet, and Toby did the same.

'Since I know you're not that keen on speaking right now, I've been teaching Juno to respond to hand signals.'

Toby looked confused, which wasn't surprising, since he wasn't quite five years old.

'First, we are going to throw Juno his favourite toy.' Sam handed it to Toby and indicated that he should fling it away from him. Juno's eyes were fixed on the toy and he bounded after it dramatically, even though Toby only threw it a short distance.

'Right; now I want you to reach out your hand, with your palm down.' Sam showed him and Toby, his face creased in concentration, followed suit. Juno was playing with the toy, but brought it back and dropped it at Toby's feet, waiting for another throw.

'Okay, Toby, give it a go. Juno should always sit before you play with him.' Toby nodded, then held out his arm with his palm down, and Juno executed a very elegant sit.

Toby's eyes went wide with surprise and he turned to look at his dad. This time, he was definitely smiling. Henry and Jean smiled back before giving Toby a round of applause.

'Now, Toby, when Juno does something right, it's really important that you praise him.'

Toby's face was a question mark.

'Give him a really big fuss,' Sam said conspiratorially.

Toby launched himself forward, and

then it was a mess of small boy and very happy dog. Sam tried to remove the 'told you so' look from her face as she turned around, but she needn't have worried: for the first time since she had met Henry, he looked vaguely impressed.

'Hand signals?' he asked, now looking slightly embarrassed.

Sam returned to her seat and picked up her mug of tea.

'It's common practice with deaf dogs or deaf owners. I thought it would be a good thing to teach Juno until Toby finds his voice. I'll train him to respond to both. We want to make sure he responds to your commands too.' Sam looked up in time to see Henry swallow nervously.

'Would you like a turn at practising?'

Henry shook his head, and Jean gave Sam a warning look as if to say, 'Don't push it today'. Sam gave her a little nod to show that the message had been received.

'Toby, I think it would be good for you both to get some practise in. So, throw Juno's toy and make sure he sits when he brings it back to you.'

The adults sat in silence, enjoying seeing Toby and Juno playing. Sam risked a glance at Henry and saw that he was completely entranced. It seemed Juno was working his magic on both man and boy. Whatever Henry's concerns, Sam was more convinced than ever that Juno would help Toby deal with his challenges.

'Same time tomorrow?' Sam asked.

Henry nodded, and said two words that Sam had thought she would never hear from his lips.

'Thank you.'

7

Juno was making excellent progress, Sam thought. Sure, he was completely goofy, but he tried hard; and as long as there were no squirrels around, he did just fine. But by far the most important thing was Toby's obvious bond with the yellow tower of fun. Even Henry had, reluctantly, admitted that Juno was the right dog for Toby, all the while looking slightly terrified. Which in itself was going to be a problem that Sam would need to work on.

Sam sighed. She'd known when she had taken on this job that she would need to try and deal with Henry's dog issues, but part of her had hoped that he would just be won over by Juno's charm. But there was no sign of that so far, and Juno had started to show wariness of Henry, as if he couldn't quite work him out: that was not a recipe for a happy dog.

Henry and Toby were due at any moment. Sam had asked Jean to come and supervise Toby and Juno whilst she had the conversation with Henry. She had secretly hoped that Jean would offer to talk to Henry. She was, after all, so much better at it than Sam was. But Jean had given her a knowing look, which told Sam that Jean believed she needed the practice.

Sam busied herself gathering the coffee mugs and the branded biscuits that she had bought in an effort to make the meeting seem less ... less what, she wasn't sure. It seemed doubtful that nice biscuits would make it any less awkward, but right now she would seek help from anywhere.

The sound of car tyres on gravel drew her away from the speech she had practised in her head.

The door opened and Toby walked in first, his dad dragging his heels just a little. Maybe Henry had figured out that they needed to address his issues too?

'Hi Toby!' Sam said with a smile. Toby waved at her cheerfully. He hadn't broken his silence yet, but was starting to seem more relaxed and playful, just as he should be. Toby was looking around, and Sam didn't take offence at the fact that he was more interested in seeing Juno than he was in seeing her, since she felt the same way about dogs herself.

'He's out in the yard with Jean and the others. We thought you could practise out there today.'

Sam moved to unlatch the gate, which was both dog- and kid-proof.

'Hi Toby! Good to see you,' Jean called, and Sam knew he was in safe hands. When she turned, Henry was looking anxiously over the gate.

'Toby will be fine. Jean will keep a close eye on him.'

Henry said nothing.

'I thought we could have a quick chat, about Juno's progress, and . . . a few other bits,' she added, somewhat lamely. 'In here, of course,' she added, seeing Henry's expression. She gestured to the sofa and he took a seat whilst she prepared some coffee.

'Juno is doing really well with all the basic commands. I think it might be good to do a trial with the school in the next few weeks.'

'The headteacher, Mrs Robinson, says that Juno will need to have passed the Accredited Assistance Dog programme before the Education Authority will sign off on him being in school with Toby.'

San nodded; she had expected this.

'I thought as much. It's not a problem, but it's important you understand that it is not just Juno who needs to be assessed, but Toby too.'

'Toby has been practising at home with a stuffed toy animal,' Henry said, laughing just a little. 'He's pretty committed to the cause.'

'I'm not worried about Toby . . . ' Sam said, wondering how best to say what she needed to.

'Juno?' Henry asked with a frown. 'I thought you said he was doing well?'

There was an undertone to Henry's voice that was almost accusing.

'I'm not worried about Juno either,' Sam said, taking a deep breath so that she could push away the surge of anger. Henry hadn't got the hint.

'I'm worried about you,' she blurted out, and then winced before reaching for a biscuit. She took a bite before she could say anything more.

'Me?' Henry shook his head. 'What have I got to do with Toby and Juno?'

He sat back on the sofa and crossed both his legs and arms. Sam was not expert in human body language, but even she could see that he didn't want to hear what she was about to say.

'This will only work,' she said slowly, 'if you are able to interact with Juno yourself. Since Toby is so young, we will need you to be able to work with him too.'

Henry's face blanched.

'There is no way Juno will get signed off if you can't be in the same room with him.' Sam knew it was harsh, but

65

didn't know how else to put it.

Henry opened his mouth. Sam was sure he was about to present a well-thought-out argument, and she braced herself to argue back. She was always going to do right by any animals in her care, and there was no way that Juno could go home with Toby if Henry continued to give off fear signals. There was a danger that Juno might start to perceive Henry as a threat to Toby, and that was not going to end well for either of them.

Henry seemed to sag a little.

'I can't let Juno go home with Toby in these circumstances.' Sam tried to say the words softly, but Henry flinched as if she had slapped him. 'It wouldn't be right for him. Or you.' She added the last sentence as a bit of an afterthought. 'Dogs don't understand when people don't like them. They work hard at first to win people over, but then they withdraw and start to view that person with suspicion.'

Henry ran a hand through his hair,

and the desperate look she had seen at the start was back. An internal battle raged across his face.

'I've tried,' he said, shaking his head at his own lack of progress. 'I even went to a hypnotherapist.' He looked slightly ashamed, and Sam imagined he was one of those people who didn't like to ask for help, especially from an alternative area of medicine. At least in that she could agree; she would have felt the same.

'Well, perhaps we can try and get you used to Juno,' she said, slowly and cautiously. She knew it was the only way for things to work out for Juno and Toby; she just wasn't convinced she was the right person for the job.

'We don't need to worry about all dogs, just Juno. He is a loveable softie. Perhaps if you get to know him, spend a bit of time with him . . . ' She didn't add 'you can get over your fear'. But Henry was nodding. Perhaps the idea of only having to learn to deal with one dog wasn't quite as overwhelming as the idea of dealing with all dogs.

'I think it would be best if we tried that when Toby wasn't around,' Henry said, his voice sounding dry. He looked up at her for the first time. 'I don't want him to be worried about it,' he added, and it was a plea.

One-on-one with Henry, trying to get him over his irrational fear of dogs, was not exactly what Sam had had in mind, but she had promised herself that she would do what it took to help Toby and Juno. And if that was it, then she would just have to bite the bullet, and possibly do a search on 'irrational fears' on the internet.

8

Sam had suggested that the 'introduction' work begin as soon as possible. She felt like calling it therapy, since that was what it seemed to be, but didn't think Henry would appreciate the term. She had done some research, and was really none the wiser as to why Henry had such an intense fear of dogs. He had never mentioned any particular incidents, which meant she was going to have to ask him — and that seemed to be overstepping from professional to personal, which was not exactly Sam's comfort zone. But without knowing why Henry was scared of dogs, Sam thought it would be difficult to fix the problem.

Henry had asked to come and visit during his lunch break from work. He said it was the best time for him, so that he didn't have to be away from Toby any more than necessary.

When Henry arrived, he was dressed in a three-piece suit; Sam, who knew nothing about clothes, thought it looked expensive. He had a sharp silk tie held together with a silver tie clip, and his shirt was the sort that required cufflinks. Sam knew she was staring; she also knew that her mouth was hanging open. She couldn't help it. Who in their right mind would wear a suit to meet a dog? A small voice noted that Henry looked extremely handsome, and this was followed by a stab of worry. Surely Henry hadn't dressed up for her benefit?

'Sorry I'm later than planned. My meeting went on longer than I thought it would,' Henry said, making no reference to his suit. If Henry was happy to ignore the fact that he couldn't be more inappropriately dressed unless he'd decided to wear a furry squirrel costume, then she wasn't going to comment either. She wondered if he was one of those sorts of men, the sort she had read about in Jean's magazines, that liked to be complimented on their looks. If he was, then he was out of luck with Sam, who thought that what was inside was far more important.

Henry looked at his watch in a very unsubtle effort to get Sam back to reality. If he had noticed her distraction, he said nothing. Maybe he was used to having that effect on women.

'Right. Why don't you take a seat in the therapy room? I'm going to go and get Juno. I'll have him on a lead the whole time.'

Henry swallowed, but nodded, and did as he was asked. Sam went to the back gate and called Juno's name. Juno looked up from the latest hole he was excavating and trotted over.

'This is important, Juno. You and Henry need to at least figure out a way to coexist.'

Juno made a grumbling growl sound, and Sam sighed.

'I'm not saying it's your fault.' Juno's eyebrows lifted on his doggy face. 'I never said it was your fault. We talked about this. There are some people, some very odd people, who are afraid of dogs.'

Juno looked vaguely insulted, and Sam reached down with a hand to ruffle the top of his head.

'I know, bud, I know. But just remember, it's not about you; and if you want to live with Toby, we've gotta figure this one out.' Sam could have sworn that Juno's shake of his head was a nod of agreement.

'Right, remember: nice and calm, buddy. Nice and calm.'

Sam clicked the lead onto Juno's collar and they walked slowly to the door of the therapy room. She put one hand on the door handle and took a deep breath. Juno was sat to heel, staring up at her.

'Here we go,' Sam whispered, and opened the door.

Henry was sat on one of the plastic chairs, looking as if he were trying to give the impression he was feeling completely relaxed. Unfortunately, even to Sam, who was usually oblivious to these things, he was failing miserably. Sam moved one of the other chairs so that she and Juno would be as far away from Henry as humanly possible, short from being in a different room altogether. Henry was gripping the sides of the chair so hard that his knuckles had gone white.

Jean had suggested that for the first session Sam just make small talk with Henry with Juno in the room. Easy for Jean to suggest, since she was a master at small talk, and Sam was fairly useless. What was she supposed to talk about? It wasn't like they had anything in common.

'How's Toby?' Sam asked, remembering one of the topics that Jean had suggested.

'He's doing better, I think,' Henry said, without taking his watchful gaze from Juno, who was now lying on his side by Sam's feet.

'That's good,' Sam said, trying a smile as she thought desperately for something else to say.

The silence that passed between them wasn't the comfortable, companionable kind. It was the awkward silence that came when one person had no idea what to say, and the other was too focused on the scary monster in the room. Sam watched Henry trying to figure him out. He seemed so in control of all areas of his life, except for Toby's condition, and apparently dogs.

'Why are you so afraid of dogs?' Sam said, and then put a hand to her mouth. This was one of her many problems. Sometimes the things that she thought just spilled out before she realised what was happening. Henry stared, but Sam couldn't make out what he was thinking.

'I mean, did you get bitten once or something?'

A lot of the stories Sam had read on the internet had suggested that dog bites in childhood could leave long-lasting trauma. Sam blamed the owners; only dogs who were scared out of their wits lashed out like that, and that was down to the owner not making the dog feel safe and secure. Even the thought of it made her mad.

'Bitten, no.' Henry looked horrified at the very suggestion.

'Then what?' Sam asked, not bothering to keep the exasperation from her voice. If he had been bitten as a child, then maybe she could understand his reaction; but if it wasn't that, she couldn't imagine what it was.

'You wouldn't understand,' Henry said, as if that were an end to the subject, but Sam was now determined.

'Try me.'

Henry stared at her long enough to make her squirm in her seat. Juno looked up expectantly and she reached down to smooth his head.

'You have to promise me something.'

Sam shrugged; she couldn't guess where all this was going.

'You're not allowed to laugh.'

Sam could feel the surprise show on her face.

'Why would I laugh?'

75

Henry mumbled something like, 'Everyone else does.' And for a moment Sam caught a glimpse of a much younger Henry.

'I promise,' she said solemnly as she bit the inside of her mouth to keep the smile from her face, feeling like whatever he said now, she might still laugh, purely because he had told her not to. She had had that issue since she was a little girl, laughing when she shouldn't. She shuddered a little at the memories.

'My mum had a great-aunt,' Henry said, directing his speech at the side window. Sam waited; she still couldn't guess where this was going.

'We weren't allowed to play with any of her ornaments, and one day I accidentally knocked one off the side.'

Sam raised an eyebrow, and Henry must have picked up on it.

'I know. You look like my mother did. I should never have been looking at it, but I was a kid and just curious.'

'Okay . . . ' Sam prompted, wondering if Henry was about to share some very traumatic childhood issue.

'Great-Aunt Bet was so angry that she set her dogs on me.'

Sam leaned back in her chair and couldn't help but look shocked.

'What do you mean, set them on you?' This was worse than she had imagined.

'They did whatever she told them to do. They were all snappy mouths and barking. I took one look at them and ran.' Henry shifted in his seat and cast a wary glance at Juno, who was showing no interest in Henry's story.

'They chased me round the garden and up a tree. One of them got hold of my trousers and nearly pulled me out.'

Sam blinked. Who did that sort of thing?

'Great-Aunt Bet was pretty old-fashioned, and she seemed to think the punishment fitted the crime. She left the dogs prowling at the bottom of the tree until my mum came to collect me.'

Sam's eyes went wide. 'And how long was that?'

'I was up there for nearly four hours, but it felt like weeks.'

Sam took a moment to take all this in.

'Wow, that's awful.' She could feel Henry's eyes on her face; looking, no doubt, for any sign that she found the event amusing. 'And it kind of makes sense of your reluctance to be around dogs.'

'You're the first person I've told who hasn't laughed,' Henry said.

'Why would I laugh? That's not even remotely funny.'

Henry shifted in his seat, and Sam knew there was more to the story.

'You may think differently when I tell you what sort of dogs my great-aunt had.'

'I don't see how that makes much of a difference.'

'They were Yorkshire Terriers.'

9

Sam nodded and returned to biting the inside of her cheek. Yorkshire terriers weren't much bigger than the average guinea pig, and it was difficult to see how they could be so terrifying to a child as to turn them into such a wreck around dogs as an adult.

'They were like miniature demons,' Henry said, with such earnestness that Sam nodded and worked to keep her face blank.

'I know you're laughing,' Henry said coldly, as if she had just insulted him in the worse way possible.

'No,' Sam said firmly, 'I'm really not.' But in truth she was, on the inside. This was going to be quite a story to tell Jean later. 'It makes sense that dogs wouldn't be your favourite creatures after an event like this.'

Henry looked at her suspiciously

scanning her face for any sign that she was mocking him.

'So, do you think the problem is them chasing you?' Sam had known other people paralysed by the fact that some dogs, those who hadn't been properly trained, like to jump up. It was just a dog's way of greeting, but Sam could understand that with some of the bigger breeds it could be a little scary.

'That and the yapping and the snarling and their claws scrabbling at me.'

Sam stared. This man had it bad.

'Okay,' she said, as her mind raced for something sensible to say. 'Well, Juno is doing none of those things right now.'

'But he has his eye on me, like he's waiting to pounce.'

Sam looked from Henry's face — which showed no trace of humour — to Juno, who was laid on his side and snoring softly.

'Well, I think maybe one of the first things we should talk about is how to read a dog's behaviour. Maybe if you understand that you will feel more comfortable.'

Henry nodded like he knew it was expected, but was completely unconvinced.

'Dogs will give you very clear indications that they aren't happy,' Sam started.

'I think I've got that bit down, thanks,' Henry said, and there was a trace of sarcasm in his voice.

Sam sighed inwardly; this was not going to be easy. Dogs were so much more straightforward.

'Fine. Well, let's look at Juno here. What do you think his body language is telling you?'

Henry screwed up his eyes in suspicion.

'Like he's trying to lull me into a false sense of security.'

Sam laughed out loud. She couldn't help it. It just kind of escaped before she had the chance to realise what she was doing.

'Sorry,' she said, holding a hand over her mouth to hold back any further inappropriate bursts of humour. Henry didn't look particularly cross, more like he was just used to it.

'Do you listen to yourself?' Sam said, and then winced, knowing it was the wrong thing to say. Why did she always put her foot in it?

'You sound like my sister,' he mumbled, staring at his feet. Sam personally thought he sounded like a teenager, but thought it was probably best to keep that to herself.

'Right, well. Let's forget about all that. What matters is, we need — Toby needs — you to deal with this,' Sam said, trying not to focus on the ridiculousness of a man terrified of dogs due to an incident with some of the world's smallest breeds. Sam herself was afraid of sharks, so who was she to judge? Of course, sharks did occasionally bite people, so that was a slightly more rational fear.

'Let's go back to Juno. Lying on his

82

side means that he's comfortable and relaxed.'

Henry looked less than convinced.

'Any time a dog shows you their belly, it means they are comfortable. They are showing you their most vulnerable area.'

Henry nodded, so at least he was paying attention.

'As you can hear, he is snoring, which means he's asleep.' Sam felt like she was trying to explain the basics of dog behaviour to a three-year-old. 'Again, this is a sign that he is relaxed and happy.'

Sam moved out of the chair so that she was kneeling beside Juno.

'Hey boy,' she said softly. 'Just like with people, it's a good idea to warn them before you approach them when they are asleep. Dogs don't like to be surprised any more than we do.' With that, she held her hand out to Juno, who gave it a perfunctory sniff and then rolled over on his back with all four legs in the air. She leaned in and started to scratch Juno right in the centre of his belly. Juno made happy dog noises.

'Do you want to come and have a try?'

Henry looked startled, like an animal that had been badly treated. She wondered if she had pushed it too far too soon.

'Okay, how about you just move a little closer to us?'

Henry stood up and smoothed out his shirt and tie. Sam once again marvelled at why anyone would wear such expensive clothing to meet a dog, particularly one as hairy as Juno, who definitely had some golden retriever in him. He took a tentative step forward.

'That's it, you're alright.' Sam realised that she was talking to him exactly as she would with a frightened animal, but Henry hadn't seemed to notice. He took another step, and Juno rolled his head in Henry's direction. For a split second, Sam thought that Henry was going to bolt for the door in his classy black patent shoes.

'He's just curious. He won't hurt you,' Sam said softly, and Henry seemed to manage to find the strength to stay in his spot.

'That's good,' Sam said, trying to sound encouraging, when all she felt was that this was going to take forever if Henry couldn't get any closer than that. 'Why don't you sit back on the sofa and I'll bring Juno to you?'

Henry backed away until he could feel the sofa behind him and sat down, keeping all his focus on Juno.

'Right. I have a tight hold on Juno's lead, so we are just going to walk towards you, and I'm going to sit down on the sofa next to you. I'll keep Juno on my right-hand side so that I'm sat between you both.'

Henry looked pale, and little beads of sweat were growing at his hairline. He dry-swallowed, but with supreme effort nodded his head. Sam got Juno to his feet, and slowly and carefully they walked over to the sofa. Juno looked slightly bemused, but a warning look from Sam seemed to have the desired effect. She settled herself on the sofa and told Juno to sit.

'How does this feel?' Sam asked carefully, not wanting to make any sudden moves that might spook Henry. Henry coughed and cleared his throat, and there was a faint stain of colour to his cheeks. Sam frowned, wondering if it was something she had said.

'Er, okay, I guess,' Henry said quickly.

'Good. Now, how about I bring Juno around to sit between us?'

Henry shifted in his seat, and Sam wondered if she should quit whilst she was ahead, but Henry seemed to remember why he was doing this.

'No, bring him a bit nearer. No pain, no gain, right?'

Sam nodded, although she didn't quite get it, and clicked her tongue at Juno, moving him so that he was sat in between them on the floor, facing out towards the door. Henry seemed to be barely holding himself in place, but at least he wasn't screaming or crying.

'Why don't you try and touch his head?' Sam said, putting out a steadying hand to Juno's side in case Henry made a sudden movement that spooked the goofball.

Henry looked at his hands and with obvious effort unclenched his fists. His hand was shaking as he reached it out towards Juno, and Sam was reminded that, for Henry, this fear was real.

'That's it,' she said softly.

Henry's hand grazed the top of Juno's head before he pulled it back. Juno twisted his head around backwards, nudging at Henry's leg. Henry stiffened and Sam reached out a hand for his arm.

'He's just wondering why you stopped,' she said softly as Juno nudged him again and whined. Hesitantly, Henry placed his hand on Juno's head again. The dog moved his head back and forth to mimic stroking.

'His fur's really soft,' Henry said. Sam nodded.

'He'll need regular brushing, but I think that should be a task for Toby.' She didn't mention the fact that Henry would probably have to upgrade his vacuum cleaner to a special pet-hair one, since Juno shed like he was getting a new coat every day.

'It's quite soothing, isn't it?' Henry said.

'I've always thought so,' Sam replied, watching the interaction carefully. 'Juno will pick up on your emotions. Since you are a little more relaxed, so is he.'

Henry nodded, and then his watch beeped. He looked as his wrist.

'I have to get back to work,' he said, standing up.

It was at that moment that Sam realised she didn't have a firm grip on Juno's lead anymore. She watched in slow motion as she made a grab for it, but Juno was too quick for her. Henry had made it across the room, and had one hand on the door just as Juno reached his side. Juno lurched upwards, front paws aiming for Henry's shoulders and doggy tongue heading for his nose. Sam shot out of her seat, but didn't make it before the high-pitched yelling started.

10

'Juno, *sit!*' Sam bellowed as she made it across the small room. Juno barked in return. Clearly Henry was the equivalent of squirrels in his mind: too exciting to worry about commands being given.

Henry was standing back against the door on his tiptoes. He had his eyes screwed up tight, but he had stopped yelling. Mainly, Sam thought, because he had realised that when he opened his mouth he was at risk of a Juno kiss. Sam grabbed Juno's collar, and with effort pulled him away. Juno looked a little indignant.

'No jumping up!' Sam hissed at the dog. 'Remember?' Juno did the dog equivalent of a shrug, and then tried to surge forward again to play with his new best friend; but this time Sam had a good grip of his collar and could hold him back.

'Why don't you . . . ' Sam started to say, but Henry must have read her mind as he was out the door and closing it behind him before she could finish the sentence.

' . . . go outside and wait for me?' she finished, somewhat pointlessly.

Sam looked down at Juno, who looked confused. She raised an eyebrow and he lay down, throwing one paw over his eyes.

'It's okay, boy. Not your fault. I should have been paying closer attention. I'll just go and sort the dog screamer out, and then we'll go and play ball.'

Juno opened one eye as if he was checking that Sam was being honest. She nodded in response, and with a huffing sigh, Juno rolled onto his side and appeared to go back to sleep. Sam moved to the door and turned.

'Stay,' she said, although it was totally unnecessary: Juno appeared to be snoring already. Taking a deep breath and a moment to compose herself, she stepped through the door and pulled it to behind her.

Sam almost couldn't bear to look, but it was hard to miss Henry. He was standing with his hands on his hips. His designer suit was now covered in drool and yellow dog hairs, and a series of pawprints marked out the shoulders. Henry had grabbed a towel that Sam had left on the desk and tried to wipe himself down.

'Ah,' Sam said, when she saw what was in his hand. 'Georgie went for a swim this morning, and that's her towel.'

Henry looked from the towel to his suit, which now had damp muddy patches all the way down his sharply pressed trousers. He then looked up at Sam, and she gulped. To say that he didn't look happy was a bit of an understatement.

'I thought the whole point of this was that you had control of that — that creature.' Henry's voice came out as a hiss, as he had his teeth clenched tightly together.

'I did,' Sam said, feeling her own anger rise. Why was he getting angry at her? She was trying to help him. It wasn't her fault that he was hysterical around dogs. 'But I didn't realise that you were heading for the door. If you had warned me, I would have made sure I had hold of Juno.'

'So what you're saying is that the only way to control him is to grab him by the collar? Yes, that's exactly the kind of dog I'm looking for.' The sarcasm was dripping off him in waves now as he threw the towel back onto the desk.

Sam knew she should take a deep breath or count to ten or do any number of things that Jean had suggested she try to rein in her temper in the past, but she was beyond that.

'Juno is still in training,' she informed him, and then glared as Henry gave a snort of laughter. 'It is not his fault that you react so extremely to him simply saying hello. If you hadn't screamed like a baby, he probably wouldn't have jumped up.'

'I did not scream like a baby,' Henry said, as the temperature dropped in the office dropped by at least ten degrees. 'I was caught by surprise.'

Now it was Sam's turn to snort. 'He's a dog, not a tiger. What did you think he was going to do?'

'Well, he managed to ruin a perfectly good suit,' Henry said, with a look that suggested he was about to demand she cover the cost.

'Perhaps you should have dressed more appropriately,' Sam snapped back. 'Or did you think that because you're afraid of dogs you were going to be immune to picking up the odd hair?'

Henry said nothing, but his mouth formed the words *odd hair* disbelievingly.

'And, if you had shown a bit of patience, I would have found my dog-hair brush, and you wouldn't have all that mud down your trousers.'

They had a short glaring contest where Sam was sure they were both trying to decide what insult to throw

94

out next. The stand-off was broken by a beep from Henry's watch.

'Great, now I'm going to be late,' he said, making it clear that he felt this was Sam's fault too.

'Perhaps tomorrow we could arrange a more suitable time?' Sam worked hard to use her professional voice. 'It would help if you didn't leap up in the middle of a session without warning.' She knew she was at risk of starting the argument all over again, but she couldn't help it: the man was maddening.

'I told you that I need a time which doesn't take me away from Toby.' His voice had softened a little and Sam joined him in blushing. It was as if they were both suddenly reminded why they were there and why it was important.

'Of course,' Sam said hurriedly, 'tomorrow lunchtime is good for me. Perhaps you could give me a five-minute warning before you need to leave?' It sounded like the most reasonable request, but at the same time Sam felt there was a risk that Henry would think she was continuing to score points.

'I will, and — ' He looked down at his ruined suit. ' — I'll be sure to wear something less ... dry-clean-only.' When he looked up, he was making an almost-smile.

'That might be a good idea,' Sam said, trying a tentative smile back.

Henry nodded. He looked like he was going to say something more, but then thought better of it and turned on his heel and walked out the door. Sam watched him cross the small car park and climb into his car. Only when he had disappeared from view did she open the door to the therapy room and let Juno join her.

'What was that all about?' Sam asked Juno as she sank into the sofa. Juno dropped his head in his lap and looked up at her with sorrowful eyes.

'Not you, silly,' she said, tickling him behind the ears and smiling as his eyes half-closed and he started to drool.

'Henry. That was just weird. Arguing like that, and then stopping so suddenly . . . ' Her voice tailed off and she frowned. What if . . . ? No; she shook her head. No, there was no way that was . . . Even the possibility made her leap to her feet, and Juno grumbled in surprise before mooching off in the direction of the back gate. He looked back at her hopefully.

'Right, yes. I have a vague recollection of promising that we could go and throw a ball around.'

Juno's eyes lit up, and he started doing a little dance as Sam reached behind the desk for the basket of balls. She pulled out Juno's favourite, opened the gate, and threw it as hard as she could. Sam laughed as he bounded across the orchard and a few of the smaller members of her pack raced in his wake. She pulled out a chair from the patio set and sat down.

'So, how did it go?'

Sam jumped and looked up. Jean was walking towards her with a plate of sandwiches and cold drinks.

'Fine, I guess,' Sam said. 'I don't think I've ever met someone quite so terrified of dogs. I think it's going to take a while.' She frowned at the thought. Then she realised that Jean was studying her with her eagle eyes, and so she reached for a plate and a sandwich.

'Thanks for this,' she said, hoping to change the subject.

'Hmm.' Jean said, and Sam knew she wasn't going to get away with it. With a sigh, she took a bite of her sandwich, trying to put the moment off as long as possible.

'So, how did it really go?' Jean asked again, picking up her own sandwich and giving Sam 'the look'.

'He wore a suit,' Sam said. Jean raised an eyebrow. 'Who wears a suit around dogs? It wasn't just any suit, either. It was three-piece, with a waistcoat and everything. It looked the expensive sort.'

Jean nodded, but said nothing. Sam

knew this trick of old; it meant that she was to carry on speaking.

'Juno jumped up,' Sam said to the ground.

'Oh,' Jean said. 'That would explain the screaming.'

'I know, right? Complete overreaction.'

'In fairness, you know how scared he is of dogs. Did you expect to cure him of that in one session?'

Sam sagged a little. 'No,' she said, sounding like a teenager. 'But why did he wear a suit?'

Jean looked at her.

'I should have had a better hold on Juno.'

Jean nodded ruefully.

'But Henry jumped up and practically ran for the door. We were just sat there having a nice conversation. I'd even managed to get him to stroke Juno, but then he leapt up . . . '

'And so did Juno?'

Sam nodded, feeling miserable. She could feel Jean watching her before reaching out and patting her arm.

'The important thing is whether he is coming back or not. There is Toby to consider.'

Sam frowned again, remembering the sudden shift in Henry's attitude. Of course that had been about Toby. What else would it be about? How could she had been so foolish to even consider it was anything else?

Jean was watching her again, and Sam knew that she had always been able to read her face, so she stood up.

'I promised I'd play with Juno.'

At the sound of his name, Juno bounded over and dropped the ball at her feet. She picked it up and threw it as hard as she could, pretending in her mind to throw away all the confusing feelings she had as well.

11

Sam had been awake half the night, and felt like going back to bed. She had fed, watered, and walked all that needed her attention, and now all she wanted to do was curl up and try and sleep. She would never admit it to anyone — not even Georgie, her closest companion — but it had been Henry Wakefield that had reduced her to such a state, and she had no idea why. He was the most frustrating man she had ever met, and his deep fear of dogs would normally be enough to put him in the 'not my kind of person' box.

It wasn't even as if she had been awake thinking about all the things she could have said during their arguments. She hadn't been searching for more pointed comments or retorts; instead, she had found herself analysing everything *he* had said. It was maddening, and in any other situation she would have sought out Jean and asked her for her insight — Jean having a much sounder understanding of people in general, as well as seeming to be able to translate Sam's feelings for her. But Sam didn't want to ask because she didn't think she wanted to know what conclusions Jean would draw, and that was somehow worse.

With a groan, she flipped on the kettle to make yet more coffee, and searched the fridge for something sugary. She pulled out a chocolate dessert and started to eat it, hoping the sugar rush would perk her up. The most important thing she needed to do was work out what she was going to do with Henry today. Sam didn't think that being back in the therapy room would be good for either of them. She frowned; she was overthinking this, reading things into the situation that simply weren't there, and it was so unlike her.

'Why don't you take Henry and Juno

for a walk around the lake?' Jean said, coming up behind her and adding a second mug to the one that sat by the kettle. 'Henry might find it less intimidating.'

Sam turned quickly to check Jean's expression. Had she guessed what was going on in Sam's head?

'You can let Juno off his lead or keep him close, but either way, I think Henry would be a bit more relaxed around him.'

Sam nodded. It was a good idea, but she couldn't help worry that Jean, as always, had her sussed out, even when Sam herself wasn't sure what was going on.

Jean poured hot water into both mugs and then grabbed the milk from the fridge. 'I'm going shopping this morning. Do you need anything?' It was such an innocent question, but Sam had known Jean since she was twelve years old, and recognised a change of subject when she heard it.

'Will you be back in time for lunch?'

Sam asked, trying to keep the suspicion from her voice.

'Not sure. Do you need me to be?'

'No,' she said firmly. 'The gang should be fine for the hour I'll be gone.' She looked Jean in the eyes, trying to convince herself more than anything, but as usual Sam was the first to look away.

'Well, I might be back, but if you don't need me . . . ' Jean said, picking up her mug of coffee and moving towards the door. 'I'm doing the invoices this morning, so I'll be in the office — unless you need the computer?'

'No, that's fine. I'm going to be working with Juno this morning.'

Jean nodded and smiled, with a twinkle in her eye. Sam watched her go. She loved having Jean living here with her — in fact, couldn't imagine her life without her — but at the same time, it was as difficult to get away with things now as it had been that night she had been delivered to Jean by her social worker.

When the car arrived this time, Sam

was ready. She had on her wellies, a bag of dog treats and everything else she needed for her walk in her pockets. All she could do was hope that Henry had decided to wear more appropriate clothing. She wondered if she should have texted him and let him know that her plan was for them to take Juno for a walk, but that again seemed to cross the professional line.

She needn't have worried: when Henry climbed out of his car he was dressed casually, in denim jeans and a black t-shirt with a hooded top. It made him look much younger than he had in his suit; and Sam had to admit that in her eyes it suited him better. As he walked towards her, she saw he was wearing walking boots, and she smiled. At least something from their last confrontation had sunk in.

Since the walk round the lake meant heading across the car park, she pulled the front door of the office open and walked out, keeping Juno on a very short lead. He pulled forward when he caught sight of Henry, but sat on command. Henry stopped where he was, and Sam gave him the few seconds he needed to compose himself. She was determined that today was going to go better. Toby needed it to — not to mention Juno.

'Morning,' Sam said, and winced as she realised that technically it was the afternoon, but Henry smiled and she pushed the awkwardness aside.

'I thought we could take Juno for a walk around the lake. Then we can practise some of the basic commands without distractions.' Apart from squirrels, she thought, and looked at Juno, willing him for once to ignore them.

'Okay,' Henry said, not sounding convinced; but then Sam doubted he would be overjoyed at any of her suggestions — unless, perhaps, she proposed that they leave Juno behind and go for a walk, just the two of them. Sam shook her head, trying to dislodge the thought, and then realised that Henry was looking at her curiously.

'A fly,' she said, hoping he would buy the explanation and not think that she had a nervous tic.

'Right,' he said slowly.

'I thought we could walk round the lake? It's one of Juno's favourite places, and we can follow a route that's a bit off the beaten track for other dog-walkers.'

Henry nodded.

'So you should only have to deal with Juno.'

He nodded again, and this time rewarded her with a grateful smile.

Sam led the way back out on to the country lane, and they had to go in single file for a while before reaching a kissing gate that would led them to the lake walk. Henry followed Sam in.

'I'm going to let Juno off the lead,' she said, looking up at Henry. 'He will usually follow his nose and won't be too interested in us.'

Henry took a deep breath.

'Okay.' Said as if he had just agreed to jump out of an aeroplane.

Sam pulled Juno to heel and told him to sit — which, thankfully, he did. She gave him her best 'please behave' look, and then slipped the lead over his head. Juno paused, then Sam waved her arm in the 'go' move, and he bounded off to inspect the hedgerow.

They walked in silence for a few minutes, and Sam wondered if Henry was thinking about their last meeting as much as she was.

'So, how's Toby?' Sam asked, partly because she wanted to know and partly because she figured it was a safe topic.

Henry gazed off into the distance.

'Much the same.' He glanced at Sam and then added hurriedly, 'I mean, there have been some small improvements since he met Juno, but he still struggles to be in school for more than an hour. He's back at home with my sister as we speak.'

Sam took a moment to digest this. Toby needed Juno, and it seemed to her that the faster they could get the two together, the better.

'I'm sorry to hear that.'

Henry ran a hand through his hair, leaving it ruffled — and, in Sam's opinion, looking better than when it was smoothed down within an inch of its life.

'In some ways, we've made more progress in the last few weeks than in the last year.' He smiled at her, and Sam could feel how genuine it was. She smiled back.

'I know that you're not their biggest fan, but dogs can transform lives.'

Henry laughed.

'I was never in any doubt.'

Sam's face registered her surprise,

'It's not like I don't see how other people are with their dogs. It's just I can't get past . . . the past, I suppose.'

'I know how that feels,' Sam said out loud, and then looked away. What was happening to her? She didn't share things about herself, and especially not that.

'Really?' Henry said, and he sounded interested. Not in a gossipy, nosey way, as other people in her past had done, but in a shared-experience kind of way. Sam wanted to tell him all about it — she didn't know why, but she did, for the first time in her life. She opened her mouth to speak but the words wouldn't come. She could feel Henry's eyes on her face and the look of understanding that crossed it. It was warm, and she felt like if she was ever going to tell anyone it would be him, but she just couldn't find the words.

'Jean seems nice,' Henry said, and Sam was grateful that he had moved the subject on. 'She certainly has a way with kids. I don't think I've ever seen Toby respond so well to someone even before . . . '

Now it was Sam's turn to show she understood.

'It's kind of been her life's work,' she said, knowing that was an understatement. Jean had a gift like no other, and had transformed not only Sam's life, but the lives of hundreds of children.

'Was she a teacher?' Henry asked, his

hand reaching out for a blade of long grass that he pulled on and held up to inspect.

'No, she was a foster carer,' Sam replied, the words suddenly hard to say. She knew that if she told him, he would draw the right conclusions.

Henry nodded slowly. 'Your foster carer?' he asked, his tone gentle.

Sam nodded. Her throat had closed up, as it always did as she considered what her life would have been like if Jean had not stepped in. Sam didn't want to look at him. She didn't wish to see the sympathy and sadness that she always saw when anyone found out she had been in foster care. She didn't want anyone's sympathy; she didn't need it. With Jean's help, she had turned her life around, had achieved so much; but somehow, when people found out, they stopped seeing *her*, they only saw a lost little girl, and she had worked so hard to leave that part of her life behind her.

'Do you think we should call Juno back?' Henry asked. Sam wasn't sure if he was actually concerned that Juno was making a beeline for the lake, or whether he was giving her the option of moving the topic on. When she looked up, she didn't see any of what she feared, only understanding and possibly respect. Sam blinked; she could feel hot tears start to build behind her eyes, but she swallowed them back.

'I think you might be right,' she said, and made herself smile before turning her attention back to Juno.

'Juno! Here, boy!' she yelled, and then there was a gigantic splash and the sound of one happy, albeit soggy, dog.

12

Henry looked at Sam. 'The obedience training is going well, then.'

Sam opened her mouth to argue, but then saw the smile spreading across Henry's face.

'It's fine, as long as he doesn't get distracted.'

'Good to know,' Henry replied, and watched as Juno attempted to swim after the ducks. The ducks themselves didn't seemed overly concerned, but there was a fair amount of irritated quacking. 'So as long as there aren't any squirrels, ducks, or water nearby, we should be fine.'

Sam shrugged. 'I'll keep working on it. The key thing is to make sure that you are more interesting than anything else.'

'And how do I do that?' Henry asked.

Sam handed him the bag of treats.

'Try shaking these, and then when you have his attention, call him back to you.'

Henry looked doubtful.

'Treats versus ducks and water? I'm pretty sure I won't be interesting enough.'

'Just try it,' Sam said; and, not for the first time in her life, wished she had some kind of psychic ability to communicate with her animals. Please come back, Juno, she repeated over and over again in her head.

Henry rattled the bag of treats, and they both looked towards Juno, who was happily swimming round and round in circles in the middle of the lake. His ears didn't so much as prick up at the sound.

'Okay, now try calling him,' Sam said, pushing her hands in her jacket pocket and crossing her fingers.

'Juno! Here, boy!' Henry bellowed, and Sam was impressed. There was no way that Juno could ignore that.

Juno turned in their direction, his

ears pointed forward. Henry smiled and shook the bag as Juno emerged from the lake like a swamp monster, complete with pondweed hanging off his tail.

Once he reached dry land, he started to pick up his pace. Sam looked at Henry, and saw his smile had slipped.

'He's moving kind of fast,' Henry said

'What can I say? I think he must have some Labrador in there somewhere.'

Henry looked at her, confused.

'Let's just say, as a breed they are motivated by food. They'll eat pretty much anything if you let them.'

Sam watched as Henry filed away this new piece of information that was not particularly welcome, and wished she had not said anything. Henry's eyes went wide and he started to move backwards, one foot stumbling after the other. Sam swung back round and saw that Juno was now bounding towards them. No, no — he was definitely bounding towards *Henry*, who had now turned around and was sprinting in the other direction.

'No, don't run,' she said to herself; and then, as Juno closed the gap between himself and Henry, 'Don't run!' She yelled as loudly as she could, disturbing the ducks, who all quacked and took to the air. Henry must have heard her, but he wasn't taking in her instruction; if anything, he was running faster. As was Juno.

'He thinks it's a game!' Sam screeched as loudly as she could. Henry took one swift look over his shoulder and Sam could see he was focused only on the large, yellow, furry lump chasing him.

'If you stop, he'll stop!' Sam shouted and started to run too. She knew it was hopeless. There was no way she was going to catch up with Juno before he reached Henry.

THWUMP!

Sam slowed to a trot. Suddenly she didn't want to get any closer. Henry was lying face-down in the mud, with Juno's front two paws firmly planted in the curve of his back. Henry's arms were spread out in front of him, and although Juno's weight had him pinned to the ground, he was using his arms as if he were swimming, trying desperately to get away.

'Juno!' Sam shouted, and clicked her tongue. 'Here, boy. What have I got?'

Juno looked up from licking the back of Henry's neck, but was not to be fooled. Henry still had the bag of treats grasped firmly in one hand. Juno shuffled forward and caught hold of one edge of the bag. Henry seemed confused by this and pulled back on the bag, and the tug of war began.

'Juno, leave!' Sam commanded. Juno stopped tugging and looked at her guiltily. Sam raised an eyebrow. 'Don't make me ask again.'

Juno looked for a split second like he was going to carry on, but then he dropped his end of the bag. As he did so, the plastic tore open and the treats spilled across the ground. Juno looked up hopefully. Sam rolled her eyes.

'Sit, and I'll let you have a few.'

Juno followed her as she scooped up a few treats, and then they walked to put some distance between them and Henry, who had rolled onto his back and was staring up at the sky. Sam got Juno to first sit, and then lie down, before placing a few treats in front of him.

'You, stay. I'm going over there.' She pointed her finger in the direction of Henry. 'You need to stay here.' Juno whined, but did the doggy equivalent of a nod.

Sam walked away, telling herself she was keeping her eyes focused on Juno in case he decided to try anything, but she knew the real reason. She wanted to put off facing Henry for a few more seconds.

When she reached him, he was still lying on his back staring at the sky. Sam wondered if she was interrupting something, so she cleared her throat.

'Er, are you okay?'

'I just got rugby-tackled by an

enormous dog,' he said directing his comments at the sky.

'I'm sorry about that. I think it was the running away. He thought it was a game.' Sam didn't really know what else to say. From Henry's point of view, Juno surely now had two strikes against his name.

Henry let out a deep, held-in breath.

'It's a sign that he likes you,' Sam tried, wondering if any of this was salvageable and bracing herself for the inevitable yelling that was bound to follow.

'I'd hate to see what he does when he doesn't like a person.'

Sam winced, and racked her brains trying to work out what she could say that could make things better. All she could think about was Toby and Juno. They had such a strong bond, and it would be criminal for it all to fall apart because of this.

'He looks happy enough now,' Henry said; he was now sat halfway up, leaning on his elbow.

'He's pretty much always happy. That's the thing with dogs,' Sam said distractedly as she tried to work out why Henry wasn't giving her a piece of his mind.

'Lucky them,' Henry said, and sat all the way up. He had his head tilted to one side, and Juno was mimicking him — or maybe it was the other way around.

'We could probably learn a thing or two,' he said as he watched Juno. Juno took a tentative step forward and then sat down again. He didn't look at Sam, though; his eyes were fixed on Henry.

'I think he wants to come over here,' Henry said.

'He does. I know you're not sure about him, but he is very sure about you.'

'What do I do?' Henry asked, turning to Sam for the first time.

'Hold your hand out and call him softly,' Sam said, and watched, holding her breath.

'Juno?' Henry said uncertainly. Juno

looked, and then moved forward a few more steps before he sat back down again.

'Why isn't he coming?' Henry asked, with his eyes fixed on Juno.

'I think he senses that you are a bit uncertain,' Sam said softly, not wanting to break the spell that seemed to be happening.

'Oh,' Henry said, and dropped his hand. He took a long, deep breath, and seemed to shake himself just a little before holding out his hand again.

'Juno? It's okay, boy.' This time his voice was steadier.

Juno trotted over and sat down again, but this time within arm's length of Henry. Sam watched Henry's face break in to a smile as he gently moved his hand to the top of Juno's head. Juno seemed to have figured out all by himself that this was a time for gentleness, and so he just titled his head to one side so that Henry could scratch behind his ears.

'I think he likes this,' Henry said, and

for a moment he sounded like an excited small boy. Juno moved in a little closer and nudged Henry, just as he had with Toby.

'I think he wants a hug,' Sam said, and then worried that she had gone too far. 'If you feel up to it? Juno will understand if you . . . '

She didn't get any further as Henry put his arms around the dog's neck and Juno leaned in, yipping quietly.

It never failed to touch Sam, the magic that a dog's love could perform. It was a miracle. Juno kept nudging at Henry, and eventually he gave in and rolled back on to his back so that Juno could attack his face and neck with kisses. Sam stood and watched as Henry laughed, feeling like it was one of life's perfect moments. She glanced at her watch. Henry was going to be late, but she didn't want to break the spell. She could feel the anxiety leaving her, and in its place settle the certainty that Juno had found his new home and that he was perfect for the job he needed to do — rescue Toby.

'We should probably be going,' Sam said eventually.

Henry tried to look at his watch, but Juno was having none of it, pinning his arm to the ground. 'You're probably right, but I think Juno has other ideas.'

'You just need to tell him. You're the pack leader,' Sam said; and when she saw Henry's quizzical expression: 'Dogs look to us to be the leader, to be in charge. They expect us to tell them what to do. In fact, when we don't . . . well, that's usually when we have problems. A dog that's insecure is likely to lash out.'

Henry sat up, and Sam wished she could take back the last sentence, worried that she had somehow broken the spell, but Henry just looked like he had figured something out.

'We need to go, buddy,' Henry said.

Juno whined, but moved so that Henry could stand up.

'Look at that,' Henry said. 'He did what I asked.'

Sam laughed. 'He does on occasion.'

She turned and headed towards the gate, and Henry and Juno feel into step.

'When do you think I can take him home?'

'Soon,' Sam said. One of the hardest part of the job was letting go, even when she knew it was the right thing to do.

'Will that be it, then? You'll leave us to it?' Henry sounded worried.

'No,' Sam said. 'I'll carry on working with you all for a while, until you feel you are ready. Assuming that's alright?' Sam felt the breath catch in her throat as she waited for his answer.

'I'd like that very much.'

Sam nodded, not trusting her voice; but inside she felt like jumping up and down, and she wasn't sure why.

13

'Today is the day, buddy.'

Juno looked up at her, and she thought he seemed a little mournful. She knelt beside him and gave him a hug and a backrub.

'It's not goodbye, silly. You're going to go and live with Toby and Henry, but I'll still come and visit.' Sam swallowed as she felt the tears building. She didn't want to cry; for one thing, it was ridiculous. She had done this many times before, and yes, it had been sad, but it was also what her life was all about, finding new homes for dogs who needed them.

Juno licked her on the nose.

'And besides, we still have some work to do.'

Juno looked the very image of innocence.

'One word, buddy: squirrels.'

Juno wagged his tail so hard that his bottom was doing a sort of wavy dance across the floor.

'Yes, I know. Their grey furry goodness is hard to resist, and you're right that one day you might catch one and make friends; but every time you see a flash of grey, you need to think about Toby.'

Juno nodded and started to wag his tail again.

'Yep, he's a lovely kid, and he needs you.'

Juno picked up his lead in his mouth and walked to sit by the door.

'Oh, now you can't wait to leave?' Sam said, finding the laughter inside her that she desperately needed in that moment. She opened the door; Juno trotted out to heel and then barked, once.

'Shotgun? Really?' He looked up at her hopefully. 'Okay, just this once,' she said as she opened Dotty's front door and watched him leap inside. Sam walked round to the driver's door and climbed in.

'But I pick the music,' Sam said, and switched the radio on: eighties music filled the small van.

Sam had followed Henry's directions, but it was not what she was expecting. Firstly, she was expecting newish, if not new. Probably on some big sprawling estate with each house the mirror image of the one next door, all large executive homes with two-and-a-half bathrooms. She checked the address for the hundredth time. This was definitely the place, but she couldn't quite reconcile what she knew of Henry with the rambling, quintessentially English, cottage that she saw before her.

It had a low-pitched thatched roof and small windows that told her it was an original. The front garden wasn't all neat and ordered, but instead filled with English wildflowers, and a lawn that was overgrown just a little. It even had the required rosebush growing around the front door. The door itself, heavy and made of dark wood, would not have looked out of place as part of a church. The roses were pink and in full bloom, and as Sam stepped out of the van she could smell their heady scent on the breeze.

Sam climbed out feeling as if she hadn't got Henry figured out at all, and for some reason it made her feel nervous. She opened Juno's door, and he jumped down and began investigating the range of interesting smells that the front garden had to offer.

Sam opened the back door to the van and collected Juno's belongings. She could have done that later, she knew she was stalling, but she needed a minute to collect her thoughts. A small voice told her that had nothing to do with the fact that she was going to have to say goodbye to Juno, and everything to do with Henry, but she banished the thought as soon as it appeared.

She walked, weighed down by a bag of dog toys and Juno's enormous bed, as the front door opened and a small blur shot out. Sam didn't need to hear the furious, excited barking to know that Toby and Juno had been reunited after their long time apart. Apparently overnight was a long time if you were nearly five or a dog.

'Hi, Sam. Here, let me take that.'

Sam had been so distracted by the reunion that she hadn't realised that Henry had followed Toby out of the door. He took the dog bed off her and beckoned her to follow him in to the house.

'Come on, you two. You can play in the back garden!' Henry shouted over the noise of happy barking. He held the door for Sam, and she wandered through into a double-height hallway that was lined with photos, both old and new.

'Head on through to the kitchen,' Henry said. 'I'll just round up the rascals.'

Sam followed the long hall past the lounge and into a wide, open kitchen diner. It was an extension to the back of the house, and the back wall was glass sliding doors. A heavy oak table which seated six was the main feature, and Sam dropped the bag of dog toys on the floor and walked across to look out at the garden, which was more of a smallholding in size. It was dotted with Toby's toys, including a climbing frame and what looked like a homemade tree house.

The smell of coffee and pastries tore Sam's attention away from the garden.

'Coffee?' Henry asked, indicating a posh coffee maker that Sam often dreamed of.

'Please,' she said. 'Hi, Toby,' she added as Toby and Juno dashed past her into the garden and started running around like loons. Sam laughed.

'It's good to see him so happy,' Henry said as he handed her a proper latte in a glass mug. 'I thought we could sit in the garden for a bit before we got started . . . unless you're in a hurry,' he added, and Sam could feel his eyes on her.

'No rush,' she said, and found herself smiling. 'My next client isn't until three.'

Sam followed Henry into the garden and to a wooden garden set. She sat down and watched Toby and Juno practise their various commands. Toby was smiling, but Sam couldn't help wonder how long it would be before he was able to laugh again, and maybe even speak.

Henry reappeared with a plateful of Danish pastries that made Sam's mouth water.

'Toby's doing well,' she said, taking a pastry when it was offered.

'He's taking the whole thing very seriously. I told him that he and Juno would have to pass a test before he could take him into school with him.' Henry's face crumpled into a small frown.

'Don't worry, we'll keep working. We're not too far off.'

Henry nodded.

'I just feel like that's the bit that could really move Toby on, you know?'

Sam reached across and tentatively placed a hand on Henry's arm. She stared at it; this was not the sort of thing that she ever did, and she felt like someone else had control of her body, especially when Henry placed his free hand on top. Sam normally shied away from this sort of casual contact. Henry's hand was warm and heavy, but it felt right in a way that she couldn't describe.

Juno's barking brought Sam back into the garden from wherever she had been, and Henry drew his hand quickly away. Sam looked at him, feeling confused and a little hurt, but she followed the direction of his gaze and saw that Toby was stood stock-still, staring at them.

Henry stood up so quickly that Sam jumped.

'Well, enough coffee. I think it's time for doggy school. What do you think, Toby?' Henry's voice sounded off, as if he was trying to convince Toby of something.

Sam looked back to her hand, and then to Toby. She saw the expression on his face before he looked away, and it caused a wave of anguish to wash over her. Seeing Sam and his dad together — not together, Sam corrected herself, just momentarily touching hands — had caused Toby pain. He had seen it, and perhaps it had reminded him of when his mum was alive. Perhaps it was a familiar gesture that Henry and his wife had shared.

Henry was looking at her now, pleading almost, so Sam stood up and fixed a smile on her face. The best way to convince Toby that it had meant nothing was to act as if nothing had happened, even if she felt a sense of loss in the pit of her stomach. This was about Toby, she told herself firmly, not about her. Focus on Toby.

'Right. Why don't you run through the basic commands and show me where you are at?'

Toby stood still and looked lost in a moment in time. Sam's heart clenched once again at the thought that she might be the cause of him taking a step backwards, of him retreating further away from life and his dad. She wanted to say something, to try and explain that it was nothing, but she wasn't sure he would believe her.

Juno barked and leaned into Toby, and finally the boy seemed to rejoin them in the present. He ruffled the top of Juno's head, and it seemed to bring him some calm and reassurance. Toby lifted his hand to do the 'sit' command, and Juno did as he was told.

Sam could feel Henry's eyes on her, and all she wanted to do was to run away and hide. Somewhere quiet, where she could work out the tangle of feelings that felt like it was pulling her in a hundred different directions . . . but she knew she couldn't. She had a job to do, and she needed to do it.

'That's great, Toby. Now try the 'send away' command.'

Toby looked up at her and Sam smiled back, trying to convey everything she wanted to tell him in that one expression. Toby's gaze was that of

134

someone much older, searching and direct, but eventually he looked away, and with his hand sent Juno away. Then, when Juno had turned, he gave the 'lie down' command.

'That's great, Toby!' And Sam knew she was trying too hard. 'Juno's really focused on you now. Now try 'recall'.'

Sam took in a breath to steady herself, and fixed her eyes on Juno. This was her job, to get Juno and Toby ready to take the assistance dog test. Once she had achieved that, she could go back to her uncomplicated life where all she had to worry about was rescuing dogs, not people.

14

Sam had suggested that she visit on alternate days, using the excuse that Toby and Juno were far enough along now that they could practise well enough without her. It was an excuse, and she knew it. She also felt guilty. There was a risk that it would slow down Juno's progress, and that in turn would affect Toby's recovery too; but Sam knew she needed space, space away from Henry.

As she had driven back from Henry's house, all she could think of was how it felt to have his hand over hers. Normally she would shake off that kind of protective gesture, but this had felt like so much more, which was another reason that she was sure she was reading too much into it.

From Toby's reaction, it had been something that his parents did, and so it was likely that Henry had done it unconsciously, which meant that it was all about his wife and nothing to do with her. Not to mention the fact that both Toby and Henry were clearly not ready to move on. All she was doing, she decided with a sigh, was saving up heartache. Heartache that she didn't need. She had survived — no, thrived — this long without any romantic entanglement, so she could continue to do so.

Her phone rang, and she forced herself to focus on work. She had the diary out in front of her, and a couple of new clients in the way of rescued dogs that need behavioural assessments before they could go up for rehoming.

'Sam Fletcher,' she answered in her best professional voice.

'Sam, it's Henry.' Sam's heart leapt at the sound of his name, but then sank as she heard his tone.

'Is everything alright? Juno? Toby?'

'Everything's fine.' He paused. 'Well, sort of. I was wondering if we could meet. I know you're not due to visit until tomorrow, but I was hoping to speak to you without Toby around. I was going to take Juno for a walk at lunchtime — perhaps you could join us?'

Now it was Sam that paused. It was probably best if she said no. Things had become complicated enough without them planning to meet up. Distance was probably the best thing.

'Please?' Henry's voice sounded in her ear.

'Of course,' Sam said. 'What time?'

By the time Henry arrived, Sam had completed all the jobs she had set for the day in record time. Keeping busy seemed to be the best approach, so she had worked like a whirlwind. Sam was just pulling on her walking boots when Henry walked through the door. Juno was hot on his heels, and charged past him to greet Sam.

'Hey, buddy!' she said. She couldn't help smiling. Whatever Henry had to say, there was nothing like a dog who was happy to see you. 'I hope you're behaving yourself,' she added, and Juno looked away.

'What did you do?' Sam asked, tickling him under the chin so he had to look up, which he did with a decidedly shifty expression on his face.

'He may have chewed a few things,' Henry said. Sam looked up, frowning.

'Really? He never seemed much of a chewer with me.'

'I have a hole in the kitchen wall that says differently.'

Sam's eyes went wide. 'The kitchen wall?'

Henry shrugged. Considering what he had just shared, he didn't look overly bothered — which had the opposite effect on Sam. If he wasn't fussed that his new dog had managed to cause hundreds of pounds of damage to his cottage, which was a listed building, then whatever he had to say must be serious.

'Oh, Juno! Why on earth did you do that?'

'I think he objected to his accommodation being separate from Toby's.'

'Ah,' Sam said, standing back up.

'It's fine,' Henry said with a shrug. 'He now sleeps in Toby's room, which is what they both wanted.' Henry smiled, but he was distracted, and Sam suddenly wished he would just say whatever he'd come to. 'Shall we go? I have a meeting this afternoon, and I need to drop Juno back off with my sister.'

'Sure,' Sam said, picking up her keys and locking the office door behind her. 'Did Toby manage to stay at school today?'

Henry shook his head. 'Managed an hour, then my mum had to go and collect him. I picked Juno up from home and said I would drop him over when we'd had a walk.'

Sam thought he was going to say more, but Henry fell silent, and she didn't know what to say. They walked in silence back down the lane and through the gate that led to the lakes.

'No swimming,' Henry said to Juno,

as he gave the hand signal that he was free to go for a run. Juno trotted off and then looked back.

'Fine. Chase squirrels if you must, just don't get wet. The seat cover I ordered for the car hasn't arrived yet.'

Sam tried and failed to hide her smile. The first few times she had seen Henry, he had looked at her with undisguised scorn when she had had conversations with Juno. Henry obviously noticed.

'I know, I know. When I first saw you having conversations with him, I thought you were a little crazy, but now I kind of get it. I have whole long conversations with him sometimes.' Henry glanced across at her. 'Of course, it's entirely possible I've gone a little crazy too.'

'Don't worry about it. It's very common in dog owners.'

Henry looked ahead to where Juno was determinedly digging a hole in the middle of a grassy area for no apparent reason.

'Who would have thought it? Me, a dog owner.'

'If you give them a chance, they will pretty much always win you over.'

Henry let his hand drop and ran it through the tall grass that lined the path.

'He had me from the moment I saw Toby with him. I just didn't want to admit it.'

Sam smiled. She had suspected as much, but was surprised to hear him say it out loud.

'He has changed our lives,' Henry said, and Sam saw that all-too-familiar look in his eyes when he looked at Juno, who was now sat proudly in his hole as if it were a fort. They walked together, side by side, in silence, but this time it was the comfortable kind. Sam had no urge to fill in the blanks, just allowing herself a moment to enjoy Henry's company.

'He's not the only one who has changed our lives, my life,' Henry said, and Sam swore she had imagined it. Henry was looking off into the distance and he made no sign that he had

142

broken the silence. She shook herself; she had promised herself she wouldn't let her imagination run away like this, it would only cause her pain later.

'After Beth died, I didn't think that . . . ' He started to say the words, and then shook his head as if he knew he shouldn't utter them. 'I mean, after she died, I was completely lost. It took me months to realise that Toby was lost too, but more than that he was withdrawing and getting further and further away from me and the rest of the world.'

Sam wanted to reach for his hands and pull him into a hug. She couldn't imagine that kind of pain; even listening to Henry recall it was almost beyond what she thought she could bear. But she knew that she shouldn't, and so stuffed her hands into the pockets of her jeans to help avoid the temptation.

'If I had noticed sooner, if had been able to see beyond myself, perhaps I could have got him the right help and prevented this from happening.' He waved his hands in the air.

'Not that I'm sorry that it has brought Juno in our lives, or anything,' he added hurriedly, and so Sam smiled and nodded to show that she understood. What parent wouldn't want to protect their child from harm? She felt the same way about animals.

Henry had stopped walking, and it took Sam a few paces to realise it. She turned slowly, knowing that whatever Henry needed to say, he was about to say it.

'I can't do that to him again. I can't. Whatever my feelings, I have to put him first.' He ran a hand through his hair and closed his eyes.

'I understand,' Sam said; and she did, however much it hurt. There had been the faintest hope in her heart that she had imagined the connection she felt with Henry, or the fact that perhaps he felt it too; but that flame had just been extinguished, and Sam had to bite the inside of her cheek to prevent the tears from flowing.

15

'Henry,' she said. The look on his face made her want to run to him, but she stopped herself. 'I do understand; really, I do. Toby must come first. I like you — ' She knew that was a lie, right there and then. She knew it was so much more than that. ' — but right now you need to focus on Toby. Sometimes things just aren't meant to be.'

A flash of relief crossed Henry's face, and for Sam that brought on the worst pain of all. She had seen it before when her life had consisted of move after move to new families, all of whom had seemed pleased to see her arrive, but equally relieved when she moved on to be someone else's problem. That was, until she had arrived on Jean's doorstep.

Henry's face was now all regret, but

that didn't matter to Sam. She had seen that too many times before.

'Honestly, it's fine,' Sam said again, aware that she was repeating herself.

Henry managed a smile.

'But we'll still see you tomorrow after school?' he said, in a way that suggested he knew that he was asking a lot.

'Of course,' Sam said. 'I still have a job to do.' It was the last thing that she wanted to say but she knew she needed to. It was true, of course; she did have a job to do and she needed to follow it through, for Juno's sake as much as Toby's. But a huge part of her wanted to run and keep running so that she would never have to see Henry's face again.

'We should be getting back,' Sam said hurriedly, concerned that she might lose all self-control if she had to stay in Henry's company much longer. She had never let anyone ever see how much they hurt her. She had always managed to say goodbye with the appropriate amount of gratefulness and used that as a shield to cover her feelings. Sam knew that her shield might collapse at any moment.

Henry nodded and called Juno, who for once came promptly. They walked back to Sam's together in silence. After all, Sam thought, there wasn't much more to say now.

'Four o'clock tomorrow?' Sam asked, knowing full well that was the time they had arranged, but she needed Henry to go and he seemed to want to linger.

'Yes, if that's still okay?' he asked, and Juno looked up at him. Perhaps he was having the same thoughts as Sam.

'Four is fine. I'll see you then,' Sam said in a firm manner, hoping that she had given the impression that the relationship had moved back into the professional range and that she was perfectly comfortable with that.

'And you . . . ' she added, reaching down to scratch Juno's ears. 'No more destructo-dog. Okay?'

Juno wriggled on the spot, which Sam took as his agreement, and Henry seemed to interpret as meaning it was time for them to go.

'See you tomorrow,' Henry said, and turned and walked away. Sam closed the door behind him, and didn't watch as he got in the car and drove off. Instead, she stumbled across the office and opened the back gate before throwing herself down onto the small step.

Georgie appeared out of nowhere and started to lick Sam's face, where the tears were flowing freely now.

'It's okay, Georgie. I'm just being silly. Let my imagination run away with me. I should know better than that.'

Georgie whined and laid her head in Sam's lap, looking up at her with such understanding that a fresh wave of tears began and Sam could feel her body start to shake with the held-in sobs. She buried her face in Georgie's thick fur and let herself cry. She didn't, normally. Usually she would do anything to keep from crying. It was a weakness that she had forced herself to stop indulging in when she was much younger than she was now. Tears didn't change anything, she remembered telling herself fiercely, glaring at her own reflection in the mirror of yet another new home's bathroom. They only made people feel sorry for you, and that never helped anyone.

Sam looked up as sandaled feet came into view. She sniffed and wiped a hand across her face, but knew it was pointless. Jean had a radar that went beyond outward signs, so she always knew when Sam was upset, even when she refused to admit it — and there was no point in doing that now. It was written all over her face. Jean eased herself down onto the step beside Sam, and Georgie lifted her head to lick her face.

'Henry?' Jean asked.

Sam's throat felt like it was closing up, and so she couldn't utter a word: she merely nodded. Jean said nothing, just picked up Sam's hand and pulled it to her lips and kissed it. They sat together, the three of them, and watched the dogs play. Georgie looked up at Sam, her tail wagging, clearly desperate to go and join in but not wanting to leave her. Sam smiled and nodded her head sideways. Georgie ran off, stopping once to look back and check on Sam. Sam waved her hand with the 'go' command, and Georgie trotted off, picking up a tennis ball and then running away with it, causing the other dogs to chase after her.

'Do you want to tell me what happened?'

Sam shook her head. When Henry had first told her, that was all she'd wanted to do: to explain every thought and emotion that she experienced. But now, all she wanted to do was forget about it. To lock all of that away in the place in her head where she kept all the other difficult times.

'It might help,' Jean said

Sam rubbed at her eyes. The tears had stopped, and now they just felt dry and tired, as if there were no more tears left.

'Thanks, but it's over. There's no point in raking it up.'

Jean didn't look convinced.

'Okay. Well, then, lunch is ready.' And she stood up. Sam didn't feel like food, but she knew from experience that if she didn't eat she would probably have to talk, so when Jean offered her a hand she allowed herself to be pulled to her feet.

'Are you still going to train Juno?' Jean asked as they walked to her spacious mobile home that sat off to one side of the orchard.

Sam looked at her reproachfully.

'That question has nothing to do with Henry and you,' Jean said, and raised an eyebrow, daring Sam to argue.

'Of course. Juno and Toby will need a bit more help before they are ready for the assessment.'

'Good,' Jean replied. 'I would hate for whatever has just happened to interfere with your work.'

Jean's expression was all innocence, but it didn't fool Sam. 'Whatever plan you are cooking up, don't. Henry has made his feelings very clear.' She sighed. How was it that Jean always managed to get her to talk about something even when she was determined not to?

'I have no plan,' Jean said, holding up her hands as if she were a magician about to perform a trick.

'Hmmm,' Sam said, as she settled into one of the chairs.

★   ★   ★

It was a good thought, though, Sam decided later. Not Jean's plan, of course, but a plan. Sam needed a plan. She needed to have their next meeting all worked out in her head so it would run as smoothly as possible.

She grabbed a piece of paper and noted down all the things that Juno and Toby needed to be able to do for the assessment. She then divided it up into sessions. Four more sessions. She frowned at her own calculations. That didn't seem right, but then Juno was doing better than she had hoped.

Four more sessions and then a couple of practice assessments, and Sam could return to her old life. The life she had built for herself that made her happy. The life that didn't depend on anyone else for her own happiness, where she was the master of both her time and her feelings.

Georgie was curled up in the corner.

'Four more sessions, Georgie. I can do that. All I need to do is be one hundred percent focused on Juno and Toby.'

Georgie looked up and tilted her head to one side.

'Perhaps I need to act like Henry's not there? Or would that seem a bit rude?'

Georgie tilted her head in the other direction, which Sam took to mean, 'What do you think?'

'You're right,' she said. 'Rudeness will just make things worse. It might make him feel like we need to have another conversation, and that's the last thing I want.'

Sam sat back in her seat and stared out of the window. It wasn't going to be easy, but she knew what she needed to do. She needed to simply pretend that none of it had happened. She would be professional, even verging on friendly. Give the impression that she wasn't in the least bit upset or concerned by their last conversation. She nodded to herself. That had to be it, and she could do it — she had to.

16

Sam was glad she had planned it all out. It meant that she didn't need to do this alone. Georgie was sat in the front seat beside her, straining forward in her doggy seatbelt. The dog was itching to stick her head out of the window and do the air-surfing thing, but Sam was having none of it. For one thing, it distracted other drivers; and for another, it was a recipe for eye injuries, which Sam had learnt from a previous bad experience.

With Georgie by her side, she was sure that she could do this. It was likely that Henry would make himself scarce, and Sam wouldn't even need to say anything. And she had the perfect excuse. Part of the assessment was how well assistance dogs did when other dogs were around. The fact that Georgie probably represented everything Henry was afraid of was more of a happy coincidence, especially after their first meeting.

If Henry said anything, Sam would be able to quickly explain. She looked over at Georgie, who was staring at her, and she wondered if Henry would see through her ruse as easily as Georgie had.

'We're here,' Sam said to Georgie. 'Now, I know you are going to be excited to see Juno again, but we are here to work, remember? It's important.'

Georgie yipped, and Sam knew she was telling her to stop procrastinating. Sam climbed out of the van and walked round to the passenger door. She clipped on Georgie's lead and they walked together to the front door. Sam lifted up a fist to knock, and then realised that there was an old-fashioned bell-pull, so she pulled it. The sound reverberated around the house and Sam could hear it from the outside. She could also hear a low whine that built and built until it was a full-blown howl.

Before Sam could say or do anything, Georgie had also thrown her head back and was joining in, the sound so loud that it could rattle teeth.

The front door was yanked open and Henry appeared on the doorstep, looking frazzled.

'Didn't you read the sign?' he demanded.

'What . . . ?' Sam started to say, and then her eyes clocked the printed A4 sheet stuck to the door that said: 'Please DO NOT RING THE DOORBELL'. 'Oh . . . sorry, must have missed it!' She had to almost shout the last few words to be heard over the combined howling.

'Georgie, shush!' Sam said, and with a sniff, Georgie stopped howling. The same could not be said for Juno, who seemed to only get louder.

'You have to do something,' Henry said, and he sounded desperate, 'The doorbell sets him off, and then he carries on like this for hours. I can't take much more.'

'Okay, okay,' Sam said, holding out

her hands as she would to pacify a frightened animal. 'Where is he?'

'In the back garden,' Henry said, his eyes seeming to find Georgie for the first time, 'and I see you brought a friend.' His eyes travelled from Georgie up to Sam's face, and his expression was full of suspicion. 'Why did you?'

Sam cringed; the game looked like it was up.

'Part of the assessment is how well Juno behaves around other dogs,' she said, trying to keep her voice steady and professional and not as if she had just been found out.

'And I suppose the only dog you had available was . . . ' He waved his hand in Georgie's direction as he tried to come up with a word to describe the fearsome monster he saw before him.

'Not the only dog, obviously, but I've used Georgie on other assessments so she knows what we need to do.' It was true, of course; but then, she had used most of her dogs on assessments, and could have brought any of them

— including her miniature dachshund, who Henry would probably have been happier with.

'Well, perhaps you and your *friend* would like to go through the side gate?' Henry said in a tone that made it clear Georgie was not coming into the house. Sam sighed as she and Georgie walked to the gate. It had seemed such a good plan. It had sort of worked, given that Henry seemed keen to stay as far away from her as possible. It seemed there would be no possibility of anything resembling an awkward conversation . . . but Sam hadn't considered what it would feel like if Henry reverted back to how he was at their first meeting. And if Sam was being honest, she wasn't sure what was worse.

The howling was now rising and falling, just like a wolf pack's, and Sam had to agree with Henry: it was ear-piercingly loud and not something she could live with for long. Georgie was pulling on her lead, but Sam held her close; she wasn't going to let

Georgie run free until she had fixed the howling.

'Juno!' she said loudly, but Juno was too lost in the moment, like an opera singer about to sing their last aria.

'Georgie, stay,' Sam said firmly, and Georgie lay down. Sam walked over to Juno, aware that Henry was watching from the safety of the kitchen.

'Juno?' Sam said, and Juno did at least glance in her direction. She could have sworn his mouth pulled into a grin at the sight of her, and it seemed to change the pitch of his howl slightly.

'Enough,' Sam said, aware that Henry was throwing visual daggers in her direction — as if somehow it was *her* fault that he had a stupid old-fashioned bell-pull that drove dogs to howl for hours. There was a brief pause, and Sam thought she had done it . . . but then Juno threw his head back and started again. Sam knelt down and put her hand gently around his snout.

'Juno,' she said warningly. The

howling fell an octave, and Juno looked suitably insulted that his singing wasn't appreciated, then fell silent. Once Sam was sure he had stopped, she released his muzzle.

'I'm sorry that no one appreciates your singing,' Sam said to the dog, who was now licking her ear. 'But the truth hurts sometimes, and you can't do that every time the doorbell rings.'

Juno stopped licking her ear and tilted his head to one side in Henry's direction.

'He is pretty mad,' Sam said, not wanting to risk a glance in the direction of the kitchen. 'But if it makes you feel any better, I think he's more cross with me now than he is with you.'

Juno leaned around Sam, and she knew that he had remembered that she had brought Georgie with her. She stroked his ruff.

'Go on, then,' she said. Juno bounded in Georgie's direction, and they started to chase each other around the garden at high speed.

'Great,' Henry's voice floated out from the kitchen. 'So I just need you to be here every time the bell rings.'

Sam didn't turn around. She didn't want Henry to see how much that comment hurt. She had thought it was painful hearing his initial rejection, but at least he had been kind then; now he was just being mean.

'A more palatable solution might be to get a different bell.' Sam threw the comment over her shoulder, pretending to be focused on the two dogs. Her suggestion was met with silence, which was fine by her.

'Perhaps you can send Toby out? We need to get started, I have an appointment at five-thirty.' It was an appointment with the local supermarket to do her weekly shop, but Henry didn't need to know that.

'My mum is on her way. She'll be here shortly,' Henry said, and there was no warmth in his voice. How had it deteriorated to this in such a short space of time? Sam wondered. There was one comforting thought, though: if this was the real Henry, if he was showing his true colours, then it looked like she had saved herself inevitable heartache later down the line. She turned her focus back to the dogs.

Toby appeared before too long, and waved a greeting in Sam's direction before diving forward and giving Juno a hug. Sam could see Henry and an older lady, presumably his mum, watching from the kitchen.

'Right, Toby. Can you show me all the commands you've learnt so far?'

Toby stopped rolling around with Juno and got to his feet. Juno seemed to detect the change in mood and sat, all his attention on Toby. Sam couldn't help but smile, Toby wasn't yet five, and somehow he was taking all this more seriously than many of the adults Sam had worked with. His forehead was furrowed in concentration as he took Juno through each command, patient and focused.

Sam didn't turn to look, but she

knew the adults in the house were watching every move. She wondered what they were talking about, but then firmly pushed the thought from her mind. If they were talking about her, it probably wasn't particularly complimentary; and she didn't need to think about that right now, she had a job to do. But however hard she tried, she couldn't stop the wave of pain that ran through her, making her hands shake just a little.

17

Every session since had been one hundred percent professional. Henry was careful to stay at a distance, and Sam suspected that had nothing to do with Georgie's presence but everything to do with her. It was strange that something she wanted was also capable of causing her pain. Toby was ready, and Sam was sure that Juno was, and that meant it was nearly the end of this. Once Toby and Juno had passed the assessment, Sam would be able to move on and forget about it, knowing that she had done her job. There was little comfort in that thought, and she knew that wasn't about having to say goodbye to Juno.

But there was one more hurdle. They needed Toby and Juno to pass their assessment. Sam had arranged to meet them at the local centre, and despite how well-prepared they were, Sam could feel her nerves jangle.

'They'll do just fine,' Jean said, handing Sam her car keys. 'You said yourself that Toby is amazing with Juno.'

Sam nodded.

'It's just so important, you know?'

'It's always important, and you always get there in the end.' Jean started to collect up the breakfast things from the small table in the kitchen.

'So, I suppose you won't be seeing them after today, if all goes well?'

Sam rolled her eyes. Jean was being as subtle as ever.

'I wouldn't have thought so,' Sam said, going for casual and wondering how she had let life get so complicated. How was it that she was both desperate never to see Henry again, but somehow wishing there was a reason why she might? She sighed and shook her head, trying to clear it. The sooner this was all done, the sooner she could get back to normal and stop behaving like a teenager.

'Text me,' Jean said. 'You know I like to hear how it went as soon as it's over.'

'You'll be the first to know,' Sam said as she headed for the door.

Later, she and Henry were sat side by side on plastic seats. Since Toby was so young, he was allowed to have his dad there to give him some support. The assessor was a man a few years older than Henry, who took his job very seriously. Sam had met him before, and had been concerned that he would be a little too stern for Toby's fragile state, but she couldn't have been more wrong. He had been gentle and soft-spoken, and his face showed that he was genuinely impressed with the small boy.

Juno was on his best behaviour and Sam wasn't sure who she was more proud of, the dog or the small boy.

'They're doing well, aren't they?' Henry asked, and Sam had to work hard not to let the shock show on her face. Henry had barely said two words to her since they had arrived, and they had been all business.

'Toby's doing better than most adults I know,' Sam said

'We really need this to work,' Henry said. 'He's made some progress, but he's stuck when it comes to school, and he goes into Year One in a few months. I've been working with him at home, but it isn't all about spelling and sums.'

Sam nodded.

'I'm sure when he can take Juno to school with him, you'll see things start to improve,' Sam said, hoping with all her might that her prediction would come true.

'Yeah, about that . . . ' Henry said, leaning forward in his seat, his hands clasped together and his eyes on the floor. 'The school have asked that you accompany Toby for the first few days.'

Sam's eyes went wide. Her at school? Surrounded by hundreds of small children? To say that was out of her comfort zone was an understatement.

'Me?' she squeaked.

'I'm really sorry, I had no idea they

were going to insist on this, but they have.' Henry glanced at her briefly and looked helpless. 'It's the first time they've had an assistance dog, and they want some guidance.'

'I'm sure you could . . . ' Sam started hopefully

'They are insisting that it's Juno's trainer.'

'Right,' Sam said. 'Well, if it's a deal-breaker, then I suppose I can move my schedule around.'

'I'll pay you for your time, of course. I'm sure after a day or two they will be happy to have Juno around.'

Sam nodded, and forced herself to focus on Toby and Juno. Another assessor had entered the room, and was waving Juno's favourite toy around in an attempt to distract him. This was the nerve-racking bit: they had worked hard on this, and most of the time Juno remained focused on Toby — but occasionally, just occasionally, he would forget himself and revert to his doggy instincts.

Juno twitched, and his head swivelled to look in the direction of his toy. Sam held her breath, and she knew that Henry was doing the same. She risked a glance at him, and his eyes were wide. Without looking at her, Henry reached out and grabbed her hand. Sam felt a jolt at his touch, something she longed for but dreaded all at the same time. Juno whimpered, and Sam turned back to look at him.

Toby made the sign for him to come and he did. Sam let the held-in breath out, and with it felt some of the tension leave her. Henry's hand was still gripping hers tighter than he had before. Only when the assessor announced that the assessment was over did Henry leap to his feet, dragging Sam with him. He pulled her into a quick tight hug as he danced around, then seemed to remember who he was hugging and let her go with an apologetic grin.

Henry was distracted by Toby running towards him, and he knelt down with his arms open. Henry lifted Toby up and spun him round as Juno danced about trying to catch Toby's flying legs.

'You were amazing, Toby! Incredible!' Henry said, laughing and sounding a bit choked-up all at the same time.

'One of the best I've seen in a long time, young man,' the assessor said, walking towards them. 'I have some paperwork to fill out, and then you will get your official certification through in the post in around five days' time.

'Well done, Miss Fletcher,' the man added, smiling at Sam as he walked past and offering his hand. Sam shook it and smiled back. This was what it was all about, and she wished that she could bottle the feeling. She stood back and watched Toby and Henry together. Henry stopped suddenly and put Toby down. He turned to her as if he had just remembered that she was here.

'Thank you,' he said. 'I don't know where we would be ... ' His voice shook a little and Toby looked up at him. Henry ruffled his hair. 'Happy tears, bud. They're happy tears. I'm just so proud of you.'

Toby nodded, looking thoughtful, and then stepped away from his dad. He walked up to Sam and tugged on her arm. Taking that as a sign that she should kneel down, she did so. Toby leaned into her, tentatively at first, but then threw his arms around her neck. Sam didn't know what to say, so just hugged him back.

'You worked so hard, Toby. You deserve this.'

They were then joined by Juno, who hated to be left out. He barrelled into them and they pitched over onto the floor, a mess of people and dog, and Sam heard a sound she hadn't heard before. Toby was laughing, a laugh of sheer joy, light and giggly. Sam didn't want to break whatever magic spell was happening, but she caught sight of Henry, who looked transfixed as if it was the most beautiful thing he had ever heard.

When they were all finally tired out, Henry held out a hand and helped Sam to her feet. His eyes locked with hers, and although no words were spoken, Sam could read his thoughts. This wasn't about not wanting to speak, it was about there being no words to sum up what he was feeling; but he didn't need to. Sam knew, she could tell, and so she smiled at him.

'I think Juno probably needs to do his business,' Henry said distracted by the 'need to pee' dance that Juno was now performing. And so they followed Juno and Toby out of the centre, and Toby crossed the car park into the dog exercise yard.

'Have you got a bag?' Henry called, and was rewarded with Toby waving a small black plastic bag like it was a flag.

'I'm impressed you've got him to do that,' Sam said. 'Most kids balk at the idea.'

'He's taking his role very seriously,' Henry said with a smile. 'And he's old beyond his years.' The smile slipped just a little, and Sam had to fight the urge to throw her arms around him.

They watched as Juno, nose to the ground, sniffed, looking for the ideal spot.

'I wish . . . ' Henry started to say. He frowned, more at himself than anything else.

'I know,' Sam said, and it was true. However much she wished that things could be different, she understood. Toby had to come first, it was only right; and whatever the cost to her, she wouldn't risk hurting Toby, ever. He had been through too much in his short life, and it reminded her of her own childhood — though hers had been so different, she could see her own pain reflected in his.

'I should be going,' Sam murmured, knowing there wasn't anything else to say on the subject. You could drive yourself crazy with 'what if's, she told herself. 'You should get accreditation through this week. Then let me know when you have sorted it with the school.'

'Thanks,' Henry said softly. 'It's not

enough,' he added; although whether he meant the thank-you or something more, Sam wasn't sure.

Sam turned and headed towards her car. Henry had joined Toby and they were laughing together. That would have to be enough, Sam thought, as she risked one last look backwards. It would have to be.

18

Sam felt like it was her first day at a new school, and she had had a lot of those in her time. With each move had come another school, with new kids to figure out and friendships to attempt. She never had much luck, of course. She always arrived in the middle of the school year when friendships had been made, broken, and then reforged. None of the kids were interested in getting to know the new kid who didn't have the right uniform on their first day and who was treated with excessive sympathy by all the adults, as if she were something to be pitied.

Her stomach felt like she was on a ship in a force-ten storm. Sam pressed a hand to her belly in the hopes she could will it to stop flipping over.

'You should eat something,' Jean said, and there was unexpected sympathy in her eyes.

'I'm not hungry,' Sam answered.

'That's what you always used to say, and then you would complain that your stomach made whale noises all through the morning.' Jean was smiling, and in her eyes Sam saw reflected those past experiences.

'That was probably one of your other kids,' Sam tried, and Jean raised an eyebrow.

'You know perfectly well that it was you, Sam. I may have cared for a lot of children, but I remember each and every one of them.'

Sam crossed the space between them and hugged Jean.

'I know you do. I'm sorry. I'm not sure what's got into me this morning.'

'Your deep dislike of educational establishments, I would have thought?' Jean said dryly. 'Sam, you just need to remember that you're not a pupil anymore. You are simply there to smooth Juno's transition into his new role.'

'What if they don't like me?' Sam

asked, and Jean laughed.

'The teachers?'

Sam shook her head. 'You know I'm not good with children,' she said, and felt a fresh wave of anxiety pass through her.

'Sam, the sooner you realise that children aren't that different to animals, the better off you'll be.' Jean handed her a carrier bag. 'I was going to put it in a lunchbox, but I wasn't sure what was in for five-year-olds at the moment.'

Sam stuck out her tongue, but couldn't help smiling. Jean was right: she was making a big deal out of nothing. All she had to do was get Juno settled, show the teachers a couple of key commands, and then she should be out of there. She looked at the plastic bag in her hand. She'd probably be done early enough to eat her lunch back at home.

'Right, I'd better go. I'm getting a lift to the school with Toby and Juno.'

'And Henry?' Jean asked, her face the picture of innocence.

'Toby is an amazing kid, but he

hasn't actually learnt to drive yet.'

Jean gave her the look that she always used when Sam was being sarcastic, and Sam hurried out, knowing that she was pushing her luck but pleased she had had the last word.

Toby was standing in his front garden with his uniform on, and Juno was by his side. Juno was proudly wearing his new uniform too. His consisted of a fluorescent yellow coat with the words 'Assistance Dog. Please do not disturb me when I'm working.' on it. He looked very smart, and when Sam climbed out of her car it was clear that he was taking his new role very seriously, since he stayed glued to Toby's side and didn't run to greet her.

'Very nice,' Sam said. 'I'm guessing you two have been working on that?' Toby grinned up at her, and they both looked up at the sound of the front door closing.

'Right, everyone in the car. We don't want to be late on Juno's first day at big-boy school.'

Toby and Juno climbed into the back seat, and Toby reached over to clip Juno into his car harness. Sam climbed in the front.

'Thanks once again for doing this,' Henry said as he started the engine. 'I know it's a bit above and beyond.'

'It's fine,' Sam said. 'No problem.' And tried to work on calming the butterflies in her stomach. The last thing she wanted to do was to give Henry any hint that going back to school was difficult for her.

Sam knew they were getting close judging by the number of children in school uniform walking along the pavement. Mums and dads waved hello, and their children ran ahead. Sam took a deep, steadying breath as Henry pulled the car into the small school car park.

'We're lucky. Today we have permission to park here, but tomorrow we'll have to join everyone else and park up the road.'

Toby and Juno didn't seem the least

bit bothered by this announcement, and Sam was sure they would have both jumped out had it not been for the child safety locks. Toby was pulling on the door handle.

'Hold your horses!' Henry said. 'Anyone would think you were happy to be here,' he added under his breath for Sam's benefit. Sam smiled; it was a good sign.

She climbed out and opened Juno's door before reaching in and undoing his car harness. Toby ran around and clipped on his lead, then gave the command for Juno to climb out of the car. Sam stood back and let Toby do his thing. She was aware that a few of the other children who had been walking up to the school playground had now stopped to stare.

Toby looked up at his dad, who gave him a nod, and they walked through the small gap in the hedge to join the other children and parents in the playground. A young woman walked up and greeted Toby.

'Toby. Good to see you. This must be Juno,' she said, and Toby smiled. The young woman blinked; it seemed she hadn't seen Toby smile much before either.

'Mrs Culver? This is Sam Fletcher: Juno and Toby's trainer, and all-round miracle worker.'

Sam smiled and shook the out-stretched hand. She wasn't used to being introduced like that, and it took the edge off the swirl of emotion she was feeling just standing in a school playground.

'Lovely to meet you, and I hear you will be joining us for a few days?'

Sam smiled and nodded, not trusting herself to speak.

'Toby? Perhaps you and Juno could lead the way?' Mrs Culver said, and Toby walked off in the direction of the main entrance with Juno trotting perfectly beside him. Sam took a deep breath and went to follow him, but felt Henry's hand on her arm.

'Are you feeling okay?' he asked,

sounding and looking concerned. 'You're a very funny colour.'

'I'm fine, just fine,' Sam said, but it came out at a higher pitch than usual, and did nothing to allay Henry's concerns.

'If you're not well, we can try this another day.'

Sam tried to smile; as if putting it off would make it any easier.

'I'm not sick,' she said. 'I'll be just fine.'

Henry had stopped walking, and since his hand was still on Sam's arm, she did too.

'Then what is it? I know you well enough to figure out that something is wrong.'

Sam nearly laughed at that. In truth, they hardly knew each other at all — and he certainly knew very little *about* her, particularly her past. Henry was studying her closely, and so she tried to move away from him, towards the main entrance. She just needed to get this over and done with. Henry released her arm but didn't move with her.

'It's about being here, isn't it?' he said, and Sam froze. How had he seen through her?

'Let's just say I didn't have the best experience of school,' Sam said, and then kept walking. She wanted to talk to Henry about this even less than she wanted to be in the building in front of her. She felt, rather than saw, Henry gain on her.

'Why didn't you say anything?'

'Because it doesn't matter. It's just a few bad memories, and anyway it's not about me.' Sam was sure that the other parents would now be staring at them, especially since it looked like a soap opera was being acted out in front of them. 'Let's go see how Toby and Juno are doing, shall we?'

It was almost a challenge, and for a split second Henry looked torn. That split second made Sam's heart feel lighter. She could do this. Of course she could. Not that any of that mattered: she was going to do this for Toby and Juno.

She felt Henry reach down and squeeze her hand, and to her surprise he didn't let go. She looked at their hands, locked together.

'Are you coming, or what?' Henry asked, tugging slightly on her hand. She didn't want to, but she knew that she should, and so she tried to gently wriggle her hand free; but Henry only tightened his grasp a little, and when she looked at him he raised an eyebrow.

'What about Toby?' Sam hissed under her breath. 'What if he sees us?'

'Firstly, Toby will be too wrapped up in showing off his dog to notice; and secondly, if he asks, I'll tell him that you were nervous about going into school on your own.' Henry started to walk towards the entrance and Sam was half a step behind, making her look like a child who didn't want to go to school.

'Trust me, Sam. That, he will understand.'

19

Henry stopped to allow her to catch up, and so they walked into the main entrance, hand in hand. He seemed to know his way round as he led her down a corridor that was decorated with children's artwork of every imaginable colour. When they reached the end, he pushed open the door that said 'Mrs Culver's Class'.

Toby was surrounded by a group of children, who looked to Sam to be of a similar age. Juno was sat beside him with his tongue lolling out, and looking very happy to have so many adoring fans. Mrs Culver was explaining why Juno would be joining them in class.

'And this is Miss Fletcher, who has taught Juno everything he needs to know to be a good assistance dog. Say good morning.'

'Good morning, Miss Fletcher,' the children all chorused. Sam felt a flash of memory flood through her at all the times she had had to be introduced to a new class, and she took a small involuntary step backwards. Henry's grip tightened again, and it seemed to give her strength.

'Good morning,' she managed to say in reply, and could only hope that no one had noticed her hesitation.

'Miss Fletcher, I was wondering if you could explain to the children what the rules are with regards to Juno.'

Sam tried to swallow but her mouth had gone suddenly dry.

'Perhaps I could start, Mrs Culver?' Henry said smoothly. 'If that's okay with you, Miss Fletcher?'

Sam flashed him a grateful smile. He let go of her hand and went to stand by Mrs Culver. Sam moved slightly so that she could lean against a tray of drawers for support. Henry smiled at all the children as they all took their seats.

'So,' he said. 'You've all met Juno?'

The children nodded their heads enthusiastically.

187

'Then I guess you know that he's not just an ordinary dog.' Henry's eyes flashed to Sam's face. 'Not that there is any such thing,' he added hurriedly, and despite everything Sam had to put her hand to her mouth to cover her smile.

'Well, Juno is extra-special. Does anyone know why?'

A small girl with a missing front tooth put her hand in the air and started to wriggle in her seat. Henry pointed at her and she opened her mouth to speak.

'Is it because he's so ginormous?'

Henry laughed. 'I thought that too when I first met him; but no, there is something else about Juno that makes him extra-special.' He scanned the room, but the children clearly had no other ideas to suggest.

'Well, you all know that Toby has trouble talking.'

The children, as one, twisted their heads to look at Toby, who smiled and shuffled his feet.

188

'Can Juno talk?' one of the other girls piped up, and there was a rising rumble of whispered conversation.

Henry laughed. 'Sometimes it feels like he can talk; but no, not really. Juno is here to help Toby.'

The children stared, and Henry seemed lost for words, as if he couldn't quite explain why Toby needed the help. Sam took a deep breath; she couldn't just stand there and let him flounder on his own. She walked to the front of the class and hoped that she wasn't turning red as she always used to.

'Have you all seen guide dogs before?' Sam asked, her voice a little croaky — but at least she was managing to form words, she thought.

There was a loud reply of 'yes's from the children, and several jumped out of their seats. Sam tried out a smile and it felt okay.

'Why do people need guide dogs?' Sam asked, and lots of small hands went up in the air. Sam pointed at a small boy sat nearest her, not knowing how the 'choosing a child to answer' thing worked.

'The dog sees for them because they can't.'

Sam nodded. 'That's right. Guide dogs help people who have trouble seeing.'

'But Toby can see,' the same little girl who had asked if Juno could speak said.

'You're right,' Sam said, and smiled at her; this wasn't as bad as she'd thought it would be. 'You see, dogs are so clever that they can help people out in all sorts of ways. Juno is going to help Toby at school.'

'Toby never stays at school,' another boy said; and he sounded a little wistful, as if he'd quite like to go home himself.

Sam glanced at Toby, who was looking at his feet, and felt her heart clench. This was a hard thing to explain, but a much harder thing to live. Juno leaned into Toby's side and nudged his head under Toby's hand. Toby reached down and ruffled Juno's fur, and a small smile appeared on the boy's face. When Sam turned her attention back to the class, she could see that they were all looking at Toby and Juno, and the idea struck her. She smiled, thinking that it was exactly what Jean would have said if she were here.

'Well, you know how all the best superheroes have sidekicks? To help them be superheroes?'

This comment received a loud response, with children calling out the names of their favourite superheroes and sidekicks. Sam laughed and Henry joined in, the haunted look on his face receding a little.

'Well, Juno is Toby's sidekick.' Some of the children clapped, and a few more wriggled in their chairs to get a better look at Juno.

'That's why he wears a cape,' the same little girl said, pointing at Juno's Assistance Dog coat.

'That's right,' Sam said. 'So Juno is going to stick to Toby's side like any good sidekick. That doesn't mean you can't go over and say hello, but it's important that Juno stays close to Toby in case he's needed.'

Sam could see that she had the attention of the whole class, who were staring at her wide-eyed.

'But, as you know, a lot of superheroes work in teams, and so we need you all to be part of that team. Do you think you can do that?'

The class as one nodded, and Toby now had his head up, smiling back at his classmates.

'Well, from now on you are all part of Toby's superhero team. Your job is to make sure that Juno isn't distracted from his job.'

The class nodded solemnly.

'Toby uses hand signals to tell Juno what to do, and so it's important that Juno can see Toby when he uses them.'

The class was silent, entranced. Sam was beginning to think that small children weren't so different to animals.

'So, can we rely on you to help Toby

be a superhero?'

'Yes!' the class shouted, and Sam glanced at Henry, who was looking at her with an amazed expression on his face.

'Right, class,' Mrs Culver said, 'please find your seats. Toby?'

Toby nodded, and made his way to a seat on a table with another boy and two girls, who all looked thrilled to be on a table with him. Juno walked to heel and sat down next to Toby, leaning into him.

'Red table, please go and get your work drawers.' Mrs Culver said. She turned to Sam and Henry. 'I think we will be fine. Do you want to go and get a coffee in the staffroom? I'll send one of the children if we need you. Then perhaps you could come back and supervise the mid-morning break?'

'Of course,' Sam said, feeling like that would be no problem at all. Henry opened the door and waved at Toby, who waved back, and then went to collect his work drawer with Juno sticking close by him.

Walking down the corridor, all seemed relatively quiet, and Sam could feel herself relax.

'You were amazing!' Henry said as he held the door to the small staffroom open. It was empty of teachers, everyone presumably with their class. Henry walked over to switch on the kettle and turned back to her, leaning against the kitchen unit. 'The perfect way to explain it to the kids. How did you come up with it?'

Sam shrugged. 'To be honest, I just thought about what Jean would say in that situation. I had plenty of opportunity to watch her at work.' Sam smiled at some of the memories; no child had ever been able to faze Jean. However long it took, she had always been able to break through to them eventually.

'I don't know how to thank you. I thought I knew what I was going to say, but when it came down to it, I just couldn't speak.' He shook his head and looked at the floor.

194

'It's a difficult thing to live with, let alone explain it to other small children. Saying it out loud must be painful.'

Henry nodded, and she watched as he swallowed in an effort to compose himself. The kettle clicked, and he stood there lost in thought, so Sam made her way over and poured the hot water into two clean cups before dumping in some instant coffee.

'This has to work,' he said, looking up at her.

'It will, I know it will. You only had to look at Toby in class today. He didn't seem the least bit fazed that you were leaving him there for the morning.'

Henry nodded slowly.

'I just want my little boy back.' Sam felt the wave of grief flow through Henry like it was a physical force, and she pulled him into her arms. All of her plans to stay at a distance had gone out of the window; she couldn't just let him stand there alone. For a few moments, he hung in her arms as if he didn't have the strength to hug her back, and so she just held him. As the moment passed, his arms encircled her, and he rested his chin on the top of her head.

'I can't thank you enough. Really,' he said

'You don't have to,' Sam told him, and she meant it. Seeing Juno and Toby together was all that she needed. It was what made her job so worthwhile.

'Yes, I do,' Henry said, and his voice was stronger now. 'I could see how hard it was for you to come into the school this morning, and you did it anyway.' Henry reluctantly disentangled himself from Sam so that he could see her face, but still held her arms.

'Can you tell me about it?'

Sam was going to shake her head. It was something she never spoke about — hardly ever to Jean, even, although she already knew most of the details. She had never wanted to tell anyone until now. Looking up into Henry's face, she could see genuine concern, and perhaps the desire to understand her better. So she nodded, made her way to one of the chairs, and sat down. Henry handed her a mug of coffee and then sat down next to her, ready to listen.

20

Sam kept one eye on the clock on the staffroom wall, knowing that she would need some time to compose herself before going back out to show the children how Juno should behave at break times. She hadn't expected to cry, and certainly not sob. It was definitely not part of the plan, but Henry had sat beside her, holding her hand, and listening as she told him everything.

'I can't imagine how terrible that was for you . . . ' Henry said, gently moving a strand of hair from Sam's face. She tried to smile.

'Trust me, a lot of children had it a lot worse. I went to Jean at twelve and she changed my life, set me on a whole different path. I've no idea where I would be without her.'

'She's an amazing lady,' Henry said. 'I've never seen Toby react so positively to anyone, even before . . . '

Sam squeezed his hand. A bell sounded, reverberating around the room and making them both jump.

'I guess that means it's playtime,' Sam said, standing up and using her free hand to smooth down her hair. She had a horrible feeling that she looked like she had been crying, but there wasn't much she could do about that. Henry was holding on to her other hand as if he didn't want to let her go. Sam felt the same, but she knew they were just delaying the inevitable. Nothing had really changed: they might be able to pretend it had in the staffroom, but as soon as they stepped back out into the corridor, it had to go back to how it was.

'I'd better go,' Sam said, gently tugging her hand from his. She wanted to say more, wanted to tell him how she didn't want whatever they had to end, but it would only cause more pain and upset. What she needed to do was walk away. The problem was, her legs didn't seem to want to obey her.

The door opened and two teachers walked in, chatting loudly. They looked a little surprised to see Henry and Sam there, especially since they were standing as if frozen in time. Their arrival was enough to get Sam's legs to move, though, and she was out of the door before Henry could even stand up. She walked quickly down the corridor, not wanting to give Henry the time to catch up. If he did, she wasn't sure she would be able to hold on to her resolve.

She pushed open the door to Mrs Culver's room and could see the children had headed out of the back door to the playground beyond. Only Mrs Culver, Toby, and Juno waited for her.

'Right, Toby,' Sam said briskly. 'First, we need to take Juno for a walk so he can do his business. But you must remember to clean up after him.'

Sam and Toby walked to the door, and she pointed to the red bin that had been put in place especially for Juno.

'Then I think it would be good today if you kept him on the lead. He might get a little overexcited.'

Toby looked at Juno a little sadly.

'I know he likes to play, but he's working, remember?' Sam said softly. 'There will be plenty of time to play with him later.'

It was as if Toby had just remembered that, and so he looked up and grinned, before clipping on Juno's lead and leading him across the playground to the grassy area that had been fenced off as a small dog exercise area. The other children followed in his wake, and soon there was a crowd surrounding the fenced-in area.

'It's lovely to see him so confident,' Mrs Culver said.

'Thank you for allowing Juno to join your class. I know it's a little unusual.'

'Probably shouldn't be.'

Sam looked at her in surprise.

'I'm a fan of integrating children with disabilities,' Mrs Culver said with a shrug. 'I think it's a good thing for all the children, you know?'

Sam nodded, surprised to meet someone who held the same views.

'I think this school is the right place for Toby,' the teacher continued, 'and I think all the children will benefit from having Juno here. It's hard to teach them to accept differences, if those children who are different go to school somewhere else.'

Sam and Mrs Culver watched as Toby diligently cleared up after Juno and was escorted by a group of children to the dog bin.

'It's also the longest I've been able to keep Toby at school,' Mrs Culver said with a smile. 'So, first hurdle achieved on day one. That's not bad going.

'I suspect you have lots of other people who could use your help. I think we will be fine here, if you want to get off?'

Mrs Culver kept her eyes on the children, so Sam couldn't work out whether she had picked up on her reluctance to be there.

'I was told that the school expected me to stay for the first few days. I don't mind,' she added hurriedly, in case that hadn't come out quite as she'd meant it.

'I think Toby is doing great,' Mrs Culver said, glancing at Sam quickly. 'And I can keep an eye on things. If you leave me your number, I promise to call if we have any issues.'

Sam nodded and then reached into her bag for her card.

'I'm not far away, so I'm happy to come back if there are any problems.'

'Marvellous, but I suspect your work here is done.'

Sam smiled, even though she didn't feel like it. She didn't want her work to be done, as she knew what that meant. However hard it was to be around Henry knowing that nothing could come of it, somehow it was much harder knowing that he would no longer be part of her life.

Sam reached the car park before she remembered that she hadn't driven herself that morning. She had been so focused on getting home, avoiding having to say goodbye, only to be flummoxed by her own memory. Henry's car sat in the car park and waited. Sam closed her eyes. There was no way she could avoid the goodbyes if she had to travel in the car with Henry back to his place.

'I hear Mrs Culver has given you a gold star and said you can take the rest of the day off,' Henry said from behind her. Sam nodded but didn't turn around, needing the extra second to compose herself.

'I've left my card, and said to call if there are any problems; but Toby is doing great, so I'm not expecting any.' She looked up at him as he was now standing beside her.

'In which case, I'll drop you back at mine. I'm going to stay at the school in case Toby needs to go early.'

'Hopefully he won't,' Sam said, opening the car door.

'If he does, I suspect it will just be

tiredness. He hasn't done a full school day before.'

Sam nodded, and for the first time she wondered what Toby would say when he started to speak again. He had been silent for over a year, and from Henry's description he was a chatter-box before that. Would he need to tell Henry everything that he hadn't been able to say in that time?

'Penny for your thoughts?' Henry's voice cut through Sam's daydreams.

'Just wondering what Toby's first words might be?' Sam said, smiling at the thought.

'Well, his *first* first word was 'dunk',' Henry said. Sam turned to stare at him, wondering where on earth Toby would have got that from.

'As in, 'truck'. Or at least that's what we thought he was trying to say.'

The 'we' was not lost on Sam, and she wondered once again whether — even if Toby hadn't been troubled by their relationship — Henry would have been ready to start again. If he had been focused on helping Toby, it seemed doubtful he had ever processed his own grief at the loss of his wife.

'I wonder that too . . . what he'll say. How he'll sound.'

They drove in silence for a while, each lost in their own thoughts.

'Sam . . . ' Henry started to speak, but Sam held up her hand.

'Please don't say it, whatever you were going to say. Toby has to come first, and he's doing so well we can't risk it; not for something which we don't even know would work.'

'I was just going to invite you to have dinner with us tonight,' Henry said. 'I thought if Toby got used to having you around, then he might . . . '

Sam wanted to believe that was possible . . . but even if it was, she knew Henry himself was not ready, and also that more rejection was not something she was equipped to handle.

'I don't think that's a very good idea,' Sam said out loud, and even speaking the words was painful. In her head, she begged him not to push her to say more.

'Why not? What harm could it do?' Henry said

'Are you serious? You know what harm it could do, Henry!' Sam had raised her voice, and she knew that was a mistake.

'He's my son, Sam. I think I know what's best for him.'

'I'm not saying you don't — but it was you who said that nothing could happen between us, and you were right.'

'That was before he was making the progress he has been. I mean, look — it's gone eleven, and he's still in school.'

'And you want to risk that? After everything you've been through? Henry, you can't.'

Henry opened his mouth, and Sam knew that he would be able to win her over with his words. It would not be hard to persuade her to take a step towards something that she desperately wanted but knew she couldn't have. And now it wasn't just about Toby — it was about Henry, too. He wasn't ready, and that could only mean heartache for all three of them.

'Don't make me say it,' Sam murmured, quietly pleading with him in her head.

'Say what?' Henry asked, and some of the anger from their early meetings was back. Sam felt like she was already losing him.

'Say that I'm not sure enough about you.'

She knew that moment that she would be prepared to risk her own heartache, but not his or Toby's. If she told him that she didn't think he was ready to move on, ready to try again, she knew he would argue. He would convince her. The only thing she could do to save them all terrible pain later was to tell him that *she* was the one who wasn't sure.

'Right,' Henry said, his voice flat. She could seem him gripping the steering wheel tightly. 'My mistake.' Now he sounded like he was gritting his teeth, trying to hold in more words.

The short trip back to Henry's house felt like it was never going to end. There was nothing more to be said, so they sat in painful silence, and Sam kept her eyes fixed on the view out of the window.

'Thank you for all your work,' Henry said, his tone clipped. 'Please send me an invoice for any outstanding money owed, and I will send you a cheque.'

Sam nodded, not trusting herself to speak, and climbed out of the car. She walked to Dotty without turning around and climbed into the front seat. She waited until she heard Henry's car drive away, then buried her face in her hands and let the tears flow.

21

Sam was sat at her desk in the small office with Georgie at her feet. Georgie was lying on her side and snoring. Occasionally she would open one eye and bat a paw in the direction of Sam's feet, a sure sign that she wanted to be stroked. Sam kicked off her shoe and used her toes to scratch Georgie on the belly. Georgie rolled over and threw all four legs in the air.

'Elegant as ever, Georgie,' Sam said, and smiled down at her dog. There hadn't been a huge amount of smiling in the last few weeks. The feelings she'd assumed would pass in a matter of days were still with her, and they were a heavy weight to bear.

Sam had sent the invoice as soon as she got back to the office after Toby and Juno's first day at school. She didn't want any excuse left to think about

Henry, and this seemed the best way. Henry, likewise, must have put the cheque in the post the same day he received the invoice. So it was over. She never had to see Henry again. Now all she needed to do was forget about him. Sam had always thought she could just move on and shake off old relationships, but this time was proving to be much more difficult.

Sam's laptop pinged, which told her a new email had come into her account. She clicked on it, idly wondering if it was a new job. What she needed right now was a new challenge, a dog that needed all of her time and attention, something that might just help her to stop thinking about Henry all the time.

The email opened and Sam recognised the sender's name. It was from Mrs Culver. Sam frowned; she'd had little contact with the school, other than ringing to check in for the first few days. It had all been going well — surely nothing could have gone wrong now? She skimmed the first few lines, which were all the usual polite pleasantries, and read on to the bottom of the page.

She sat back in her chair, knowing she should feel relieved. There was nothing wrong: in fact, both Toby and Juno were doing brilliantly. Toby was managing to get through the whole school day, and had even developed some friendships. And although he was yet to speak, Mrs Culver said she felt very optimistic about his future.

It was nice to read about how well they were both doing. At times, usually in the middle of the night when she couldn't sleep, she would reach for her mobile and click on Henry's phone number, desperate to find out how they were doing . . . but the thought of how Henry might react always stilled her hand.

The email wasn't a request for help — it was, in fact, an invitation. The school fete was to be held on the following Saturday, and Juno was to be guest of honour — both he and Toby were to be given awards.

The idea made Sam smile, but she just didn't think she could do it. She would have loved to see Toby and Juno one last time, but she had no idea what she would even say to Henry, and it seemed unlikely that they would be able to avoid each other on such an occasion.

'What are you frowning like that for?' Jean asked, putting a pile of post on the desk. 'I've told you before, that's the best way to get wrinkles.'

Sam looked up, not wanting to tell Jean about the invitation as she knew what her response would be.

'Not frowning,' Sam said, and with an effort she forced her facial muscles to relax and smooth out her forehead. 'Just reading without my glasses.'

It was a lame excuse, and it was clear that Jean wasn't buying it. Standing there with her hands on her hips was a sure sign. Sam sighed.

'It's good news, actually. It's an email from Toby's teacher, just giving me an update on how he and Juno are doing.' For a brief second, Sam hoped that would be enough to put Jean off the scent.

'Brilliant, love. Let me see,' Jean said, and without waiting for a reply she walked around behind Sam's chair, peered over her shoulder, and read the email.

'They're getting awards? That's just wonderful! I think I'll come along with you. I'd love to see how well they are doing.' Jean smiled down at Sam, and then saw her expression.

'That look had better not be you telling me you're not going.' She looked stern now, as she always did when Sam didn't want to do something that Jean thought she should.

'It could be really awkward . . . ' Sam started to say. She had given Jean a very brief description of her time at the school, and had tried to skim over the details of her and Henry, focusing instead on how it had gone for Toby and Juno, but she should have known better. Jean must have read between the lines, as she always did.

'Only if you make it that way, Sam,' Jean said, straightening up, 'You have to go. Think about Toby and Juno. That boy's been through enough in his short life so far; he doesn't need you disappointing him over something like you and Henry not quite seeing eye to eye.'

Sam mouthed the last part of the sentence silently as Jean went to leave the office.

'Well, I'll be going, and I think you need to have a long hard think about your priorities,' Jean said. Seemingly satisfied with her parting shot, she went out through the back garden and into the orchard. Sam could hear the dogs barking in greeting. She leaned back in her chair and closed her eyes.

There was possibly only one thing worse than the thought of having to see Henry again, and that was dealing with Jean's disappointment in her, which was worse than being shouted at. But then, Jean was the pro when it came to dealing with human beings. There was nothing for it: whether she liked it or not, Sam was going to have to try and make the best of it.

Georgie groaned as she rolled over, and Sam knew she was looking at her.

'Well, if I'm going, I don't see why you shouldn't come. I suspect you'd like to see Toby and Juno again too.' Sam reached down and scratched Georgie behind the ear. Georgie looked up at her, and Sam was sure she could see reproach in her eyes.

'Yes, okay. Your presence would also probably keep Henry away. But I'm only trying to make things less awkward.'

Georgie barked, and it sounded a bit like a laugh. Georgie was right, of course: it was probably a bad move, but if Jean expected her to go, then she was at least going to have her loyal dog by her side.

Saturday dawned, and Sam lay in bed wishing it would rain, figuring that most school fetes would be cancelled if the weather was bad. Then her thoughts turned to Toby and Juno, and she felt bad. She slipped her feet over the edge of the bed. This was their day, and that was what she needed to focus on.

It took her an age to get dressed: she just couldn't decide. Sam stared at herself in the mirror and wondered when she had turned into *that* person. She never worried about what she wore, she always simply chose the most appropriate outfit for the occasion — but she couldn't figure out what that was today. Usually she wore jeans or cargo trousers, but today she was drawn to one of her maxi skirts. It was, after all, a beautiful summer's day, and it wasn't like she was actually going to work.

Dressed in her long black embroidered skirt and a light white short-sleeved shirt, she pushed her feet into her one and only pair of girly sandals. Sam glanced at her phone and realised that she was going to be late if she didn't get a move on. She still needed to feed and water all the animals, and that would take at least an hour even if she didn't stop to have a chat with each of them.

Sam and Georgie were waiting outside Dotty for Jean. Sam had managed to get all the chores done without spoiling her outfit, and Georgie was wearing her best red collar.

'Well, don't you look lovely,' Jean said, walking around the side of the office building from her mobile home. Jean was dressed in a long, flowy summer dress, and had topped it off with a wide-brimmed straw hat.

'Looking pretty good yourself,' Sam said, deciding to rise above the obvious hidden meaning in Jean's compliment. Her choice of clothing had nothing to do with Henry; it was just that she didn't get the opportunity to wear much that wasn't at the practical end of her wardrobe very often.

Dotty chugged along the winding lanes that took them to Toby's school. The traffic was slow-moving, and it seemed clear that everyone from the surrounding villages was also attending the fete. Sam had to drive Dotty past the school gates to find a spot to park in, so they walked back down the road with other families, all going in the same direction.

The children seemed to know where they were headed, and streamed across the playground and round the back of the main school building onto the wide expanse that was the school playing field. It was exactly as Sam imagined a school fete should be. There was bunting everywhere, for one thing. Stalls of all sorts lined one side of the field, and there was a small stage at the other end complete with microphone, plus a table with trophies on it.

Georgie suddenly strained on her lead and whimpered, and Sam knew that she had spotted Juno. She searched the crowd and saw Toby and Juno running towards them. Sam couldn't see Henry, and so she relaxed a little. Juno jumped up and gave her a quick kiss on the nose before doing figures-of-eight around Georgie.

Toby stopped short, and waved at both Sam and Jean.

'Hi Toby,' Jean said. 'You look like you've grown. Have you got older since I last saw you?' she enquired, with a mock frown. Toby giggled, and when Jean held out her arms Toby rushed into them and gave her a hug. Juno was alternating between playing with Georgie and wanting to say hello to Sam, and before long it was a mass of dogs, a small child, and grown-ups.

'Henry, good to see you,' Jean said out of the blue, and Sam froze on the spot. She wasn't sure she was ready, wasn't sure that she could pull off seeming cool and detached; but she took a deep breath and forced herself to turn around. She knew her feelings for Henry hadn't changed, but she couldn't — no, wouldn't — risk Toby being hurt by her actions. So she knew she had to accept that nothing could ever happen. But that didn't make it any easier to be around him.

'Jean, lovely to see you.' He gave Sam

a quick glance. 'Sam,' he said with a nod, but there was no smile for her. 'I'm surprised to see you here.'

Henry's manner was formal, and he wasn't bothering to conceal the hurt he still obviously felt. Sam looked down at Georgie. That was all she really needed to know about how this day was going to go.

22

'Mrs Culver invited Sam to come and see Juno and Toby get their certificates,' Jean said, in a tone that suggested that Henry should have been the one inviting her. Henry had the good grace to look a little sheepish.

'Of course,' he said. 'I've been so busy . . . '

Sam didn't have to look at Jean to know that she was giving Henry the look. Sam coughed to try and cover up the smile that was tugging at the corner of her mouth. It was funny to see someone else experience Jean's thinly-veiled criticisms. Jean was never keen to let anyone get away with what she referred to as 'nonsense'.

Henry drew himself up, and it seemed that he was prepared to take it on the chin. Sam glanced at Toby, who was looking between Jean and Henry with a look of awe on his face. Clearly he had never seen his dad schooled in such a way before.

'I should have thought to invite you both, of course. My apologies,' Henry said — a little stiffly, but somehow it still made Sam feel better enough to be gracious.

'No problem. When I got the invite from Mrs Culver, I knew I had to come and see Toby and Juno in their moment of glory.' She grinned down at Toby, who grinned back, Sam purposefully avoiding Henry's gaze.

They were saved from any further awkward attempts at conversation by a high-pitched squeal booming from the speakers which had been set up around the small stage.

'Ladies, gentlemen and children. I would like to thank you for attending our school fete today!' The tall, slender woman who Sam thought was probably the headteacher smiled down on the crowd in front of her. 'Any money raised today will be split between the school library fund and a local animal shelter, Muddy Paws Rescue, but I will tell you more about that in a minute.

'First, I would like to invite our special guests to come and officially open this year's school fete. Toby and Juno Wakefield, would you please come and join me on the stage?'

Toby looked up at his dad, and together with Juno they walked towards the stage. Jean and Sam followed in their wake, wanting to make sure they got a good view.

'Now, many of you know Toby,' the headteacher said, placing one hand on Toby's shoulder as he joined her on the stage, looking decidedly nervous. 'But some of you may not have met Juno.' Juno lifted his head at the sound of his name, and barked. Toby grinned and rested a hand on his dog's head.

'Juno is no ordinary dog. He is a highly-trained assistance dog.' The headteacher paused to let that sink in, and all Sam could hope in that moment was that no squirrels decided to put in an appearance.

'Juno is a working dog, and helps Toby at school — although he is very popular with all the children, as you can imagine.' A ripple of laughter ran through the other parents.

'Juno has been helping Toby for a month now, and Toby is making excellent progress, so we thought it was appropriate for our two star pupils to officially open the fete.' The headteacher smiled at Toby before handing him a pair of scissors. Sam could see now that a red ribbon had been stretched across the front of the stage.

'Toby, if you will?' the headteacher said, and Toby cut the ribbon. The applause was so loud that Sam was worried that Toby would be frightened; but with Juno leaning against his leg, he just gave a shy wave and then left the stage.

'Well, he couldn't have done that a month ago,' Jean said, putting an arm around Sam's shoulders. Sam nodded, not trusting her voice to stay level enough to speak. Without intending to, her eyes moved to rest on Henry, and she felt that all-too-familiar sensation of loss.

'Come along,' Jean said. 'Let's take a look round the stalls. The prizes aren't awarded for another hour or so.'

It wasn't the most relaxing hour. Sam had one eye on the lookout for Henry, and managed to steer Jean in the opposite direction whenever it looked like their paths might cross. It was almost a relief when the voice boomed out over the microphone that the award ceremony would begin shortly. Sam had planned to stay on the edge of things — she wanted to see Juno and Toby get their awards, but also to avoid Henry. Jean, however, was having none of it; and, short of Sam digging her heels in and refusing to move, like an unruly toddler, she had to give in and allow herself to be guided to the foot of the stage.

Sam stood and clapped and smiled.

It was hard not to, with all the children coming up and receiving certificates, then bouncing into the arms of proud parents. Henry was standing on the other side of the stage with Toby, and Sam wondered if he was working as hard at avoiding her as she was him.

'And now, our final award of the day,' the headteacher said, giving a small pause to allow the gravitas of the situation to sink in. 'Every year, we give an award to the student who has excelled in their personal learning journey. We call it the Star Student Award.'

The headteacher looked around the crowd, just as Sam imagined she would in a school assembly. 'This award is important because we also ask the children to vote, and this year the decision was unanimous.

'The Star Student Award this year goes to two individuals — and this is a first, as we've never given an award to a dog before!'

The children started to clap and jump up and down.

'This year's Star Student Award goes to . . . Toby and Juno Wakefield!'

Toby and Juno climbed onto the stage side by side. The headteacher handed Toby a small silver trophy and a certificate, before pinning a badge onto Toby's chest. She then bent down and put a medal around Juno's neck. Juno was unable to contain his excitement, and licked the headteacher on the nose. Everyone laughed, including her.

'So please can I ask you to clap for our very special award recipients, both human and canine.'

The applause was almost deafening. Toby and Juno climbed down the steps and were almost swamped by children, some of which Sam recognised as being part of his class. Juno was being given hugs, and in return was kissing and licking the children.

'In case you ever need to remember, that's why you do it,' Jean's voice sounded in Sam's ear, and Sam tried to surreptitiously wipe away a tear. For the first time in weeks, the tears were purely joyful, with no hint of sadness.

'Come on,' Jean said. 'We should go and congratulate the stars.' Jean slipped her arm through Sam's and tugged her to where a group of parents surrounded Henry, talking animatedly.

As Sam approached, Mrs Culver appeared to congratulate Toby, and also introduce Sam to the many parents. Sam smiled and answered questions until her face started to ache, but eventually the crowd thinned enough that she could see Toby and Juno.

'I'm so proud of you, Toby!' Sam heard Henry say. 'And you too, of course, Juno,' he added, pulling his son and their dog into a hug.

'Look, Daddy!' a small, slightly croaky voice said.

Amongst the background noise of the fete, a small bubble of silence seemed to appear. Sam stared, thinking she had simply heard another child. Perhaps she wanted Toby to speak so badly that she was imagining what could only be described as the perfect end to the day.

Henry was frowning and holding Toby at arm's length.

'What did you say?' Henry managed to force the words out. Sam could see fear on his face. Had Toby really spoken — or had Henry, like Sam, wished for something so hard that his imagination had played a cruel trick?

'Look, Daddy,' the small voice said again, and this time there was no doubt that it was coming from Toby. 'Look what I won.'

Toby was shaking his trophy in his dad's face. Sam could feel her own face crumple as Henry's did, and this time she didn't bother to try and hide the tears. She could sense that Jean had joined her. Henry lifted Toby up into his arms, and Sam could see he was shaking. She wanted so badly to join them, to hug them both, but held herself back. If nothing else, this was their moment.

'You truly are a miracle worker,' Mrs Culver said, wiping away her own tears. Sam managed a smile, and the two women hugged.

'It's all Juno,' Sam said. 'I just help him learn to behave. All dogs, they just seem to know what people need.'

'I think you underestimate your role,' Mrs Culver said, laughing.

'She always has,' Jean said, every bit the proud parent. 'I'm Jean,' she added, holding out her hand, which Mrs Culver shook. 'I'm Sam's mum.'

Sam always loved it when Jean introduced herself like that: in every way that was important, Jean *was* her mum, even if she hadn't come into her life until she was nearly a teenager.

Henry was swinging Toby around, and Toby was giggling and laughing. It was the kind of moment you wanted to remember forever, Sam thought. Juno was leaping up and trying to join in, and so Henry gently placed Toby's feet back on the floor so they could have another joint hug. This time, Henry buried his face in Juno's ruff. Sam and Jean laughed together, since only they knew the journey that Henry had been on to even be in the same room as a dog, let alone hug one.

When Henry looked up, Sam couldn't look away. Their eyes met and there was no need for words. Sam nodded as she tried to fight back the tears. She wanted to tell him it was okay, because it was. Henry had opened her eyes to what was possible in life — what she might even need and want for herself. Even if that person couldn't be him, there was no doubt that it was a gift.

Sam felt Jean reach for and squeeze her hand. Juno nudged Toby, and together they walked over to Sam, Toby looking shy and uncertain. Sam knelt down and gave Juno a scratch behind his ears.

'You've done so well, Toby. Juno looks in tip-top condition. I'm very proud of you both.'

Toby smiled, then a shadow appeared over them, and Sam knew that Henry was standing next to them.

'Toby, we should probably be going.'

Toby looked up and nodded, before giving Jean a quick hug.

'Thank you,' Henry said, and this time his was the voice that sounded as if it hadn't been used in the longest time. 'For everything.'

For a moment, Sam thought he was going to say more; but with an effort he seemed to swallow it back down. He turned and took Toby's hand, and Sam watched them walk away until they disappeared from view into the crowd.

23

It had been weeks since Sam had last seen Henry and Toby. She ran the brush down the side of one of her rescue ponies, Mac, who tried to dodge away from her. She put one hand on his back and continued to brush. Who was she kidding? It had been exactly three weeks and five days, and if she thought hard enough, she could probably work out the number of hours too.

She was making progress, though. She had gone for whole hours without con-juring up an image of Henry smiling, or Toby uttering his first words in over a year. She wondered how chatty he was now, and what he had to say. Even though the memory of Henry was painful, she could still smile at the thought of the pair of them together, thick as thieves, talking about anything and everything.

The bell rang, which meant that

someone was at the door to the office. Sam glanced at her watch: her next client wasn't due for at least an hour, so it was probably the postman or the animal-feed delivery guy. It wasn't like she was expecting anyone else. She held out a mint for the pony, who crunched it between his teeth; and then, realising brushing was over for the day, he kicked up his heels and went for a mad dash around the orchard.

Sam wiped her hands on her already-scruffy jeans and went to unlock the door. She pulled it wide open, and then stood and stared. It was the one person in the whole world she was least expecting. She looked beyond to the car park, but there was no car there, or any sign of anyone else.

'Toby?' she finally managed to force out. 'How on earth did you get here?' Sam stood back and ushered the small boy into the office. Juno made a yipping noise, and Sam reached down and stroked him; but she could feel the anxiety flowing from the dog, and she was sure this had not been his idea.

'Toby, where's your dad?' Sam asked, directing the boy to sit on the sofa and pulling her mobile from her jeans pocket. She scrolled through the phone memory before she realised that she had deleted Henry's number. It had taken real determination, but she had known it was the only way to move on, the only way to remove temptation.

'At home,' Toby said, and the sound of his voice still surprised her.

'Does Daddy know where you are?' Sam asked, knowing full well what the answer would be, but somehow feeling that she needed to ask the question anyhow. Toby looked away, but then shook his head.

'Right,' Sam said, 'I think we need to let him know you are safe.' Toby just shrugged, and she couldn't for the life of her figure out what was going on with the little boy.

'I'm going to text Jean and ask her to come up from her house with something to eat and drink, okay?' Sam asked, but Toby made no reply.

Sam made quick work of the text, and then with one eye on Toby, she went over to her desk and switched her computer on. She would still have Henry's contact details in Juno's file. She was just scrolling through when the door opened and Jean charged in, wearing an apron with flour all down it.

'Toby! Whatever are you doing here all by yourself?'

Sam didn't glance up to see Toby's reaction. She knew that Henry would be frantic, and she wanted to tell him Toby was safe as soon as she could.

'Oh, darling, come here,' Jean said, and Sam looked up to see Toby folded into a hug. 'I'm making a cake. Why don't you come and help me whilst Sam lets your daddy know that you're okay?'

Sam didn't hear an answer, but lifted her mobile to her ear. She nodded at Jean, who carried the small boy out of the door, with Juno trailing in her wake. The phone rang once.

'Sam, I don't have time right now,' Henry said, his voice terse and distracted. 'Toby and Juno . . . '

San cut him off: she couldn't bear to prolong his agony any longer.

'They're here, Henry. They're both safe.'

There was a pause, and it seemed like Henry was having trouble processing the news.

'They're with you?' Henry said, his words rushing out. 'If you wanted to see them both, you only had to ask. I've been going frantic! I've looked everywhere; I was just about to call the police.' He was nearly shouting now, and although Sam couldn't really blame him, she also felt hurt at his suggestion.

'Henry, Toby just turned up on my doorstep.'

There was another short period of dead air as Henry seemed to again be struggling with the new information.

'How did he get there?'

'Well, I'm assuming they walked.'

'It's over three miles.'

'I know,' Sam said. 'Did you two have a fight or something?' Sam frowned; even if that were true, she couldn't imagine Toby coming to her first. He would go to see his Grandma or his Aunty, surely. Unless . . . unless it was something to do with Juno.

'Did Juno do something?' Sam asked, dreading the answer. Surely Henry wasn't looking to separate the boy and his dog? Whatever Juno had done, it couldn't be bad enough to want to destroy all the progress that Toby had made.

'No, not that I know of; and even if he had . . . ' Henry's voice trailed off, and it seemed to Sam that he was struggling to understand what was going on as much as she was. She heard down the phone the beep of a car being unlocked.

'I'm on my way,' Henry said, and Sam opened her mouth to tell him to drive carefully, but all she could hear was the silence that told her he had hung up.

Sam stood outside and waited. She didn't have to wait long. Henry pulled his car into the space at the front of the office, not bothering to park it properly, and jumped out.

'Where are they?' he demanded, and Sam felt some relief that Henry had asked about both Toby and Juno.

'With Jean,' Sam said, and led Henry around the office into the side plot that housed Jean's mobile home and vegetable patch, which was safely fenced off from the various animals that lived with Sam.

Jean had obviously been keeping a watchful eye out, as she opened the door straight away. Sam could just make out Toby hiding behind her legs.

'Toby, I've been worried out of my mind!' Henry shouted and ran forward. Toby slipped around Jean's legs and threw himself into Henry's waiting arms. Henry hugged him tight.

'You must never do that again, Toby. I was so scared that something had happened to you.'

Sam couldn't hear Toby's reply, but she did hear Henry's.

'I know that Juno was with you, but you must never go out like that unless you have an adult with you too.'

Henry set him back down on his feet. Toby whispered something into his father's ear.

'Of course I'm not mad at Juno,' Henry said, ruffling his son's hair and then reaching over to scratch Juno's ears. 'You wouldn't like it if Juno decided to walk over here without you, would you?'

Toby's eyes went wide and he shook his head vigorously, before grabbing Juno's collar as if he was worried that if he didn't, he would run off.

'Why don't we all have a seat?' Jean said, indicating the double swing seat and surrounding garden chairs. 'I'm just getting my baking out of the oven. It looks like we could all do with a cup of tea and a slice of cake.'

When they had all sat down — Henry, Toby and Juno, who clearly wasn't about to let Toby out of his sight, on the double swing chair, and Sam in one of the sofa chairs, Henry seemed to think it was the right time to continue his conversation with Toby.

'I need to know why you would walk over here all by yourself.' Toby looked up. 'Okay, yes, I know Juno was with you; but that's not really the point, is it?'

Toby shrugged, and Juno laid his head on the boy's lap.

'Juno wanted to see Sam,' Toby said, his voice so quiet that Sam had to strain to hear him.

'Then why didn't you ask me? We could have brought Juno over here together.'

Toby looked at him, and Sam saw a silent conversation pass between them.

'You only had to ask.'

'You said Sam didn't want to see us,' Toby blurted out, and this time his words were much louder. It seemed to surprise Toby too, as if he wasn't used to his newfound voice. Henry's cheeks coloured, and Sam could see that he wanted to look at her but was too embarrassed.

'You know that wasn't what I said, Toby.' Toby looked uncertain, and Henry pulled him into a hug. 'I said that Sam had other people and dogs to help, and we shouldn't bother her.'

With the boy curled up in his lap, Henry finally looked over at Sam, and his eyes begged her to understand. She smiled and then nodded to show that she did. Henry, in his own way, had been trying to protect all of them from the hurt that had caused her to say those words to him in the first place.

'You wanted to see her too, didn't you?' Henry murmured. 'You should have said, Toby. We could have rung Sam and arranged a time to meet. I'm sure Sam wouldn't have minded.'

Sam smiled to show that she would have been fine with that.

'Well, we're here now. Why don't you speak to her yourself?' Sam watched as Toby shook his head. 'But you're getting so good at talking . . . ' Henry squeezed Toby one more time and then gently turned him round. 'Why don't you take Juno with you? I think he has something to tell Sam too.'

Toby, released from his dad's hug, walked slowly over, and Juno jumped off the seat and walked with him. Sam smiled at him, trying to encourage him without words.

'Thank you for bringing me, Juno,' Toby said, softly again.

'Oh, you are very welcome, Toby,' Sam said, smiling.

Juno jumped up and started to lick Sam's ears.

'Juno wants to say thank-you too,' Toby said, giggling, and Sam joined in.

'I can see that,' she said between her own giggles. 'Well, you are very welcome too, Juno. I knew you had it in you.'

'Daddy misses you,' Toby said; and both Henry and Sam froze as if it were the first time Toby had spoken all over again.

24

Jean came out of the mobile home carrying a tray of tea things and cake, and not even that could break the silence that had befallen Sam and Henry. They both sat and stared at Toby, and Sam wondered if, like her, Henry was wondering if he had imagined his son's words. Toby, it seemed, was warming to his subject.

'He doesn't say it, but I know,' Toby added as Jean placed the tea-tray on the table and handed him a beaker of orange squash.

'What do you know?' Jean asked, having missed the start of the conversation.

'That Daddy misses Sam,' Toby said, and Jean tried but failed to hide her smile.

'I'll let you into a secret, Toby — my Sam misses your daddy too.'

Toby frowned. 'I miss Mummy, but she's in heaven,' he said, and Henry leaned forward and kissed his son on the top of his head.

'I know you do, buddy. I miss Mummy too.'

'But you don't have to miss Sam,' Toby said, turning to face him, and Sam felt her breath catch in her throat. 'Sam is here, and you can walk here,' he pointed out, as if it was the most obvious thing in the world.

'It's a little more complicated than that,' Henry said, his focus flicking from Sam back to his son.

'Why? Jean says Sam misses you too. Why don't you come and see Sam? You wouldn't even have to walk,' Toby said. 'You have a car. I don't have a car,' he added unnecessarily.

Sam knew that Henry was looking at her, but wasn't certain she was brave enough to look up, not sure what she would see if she did. Juno nudged her, and his expression said, 'What's the matter with you?' Not wanting to be shamed by a dog, Sam looked up. Henry was gazing at her, and it was like he was seeing her for the first time.

'Well, I didn't realise that Sam wanted to see me,' Henry said, his eyes fixed on Sam's face; and Sam knew she didn't need to say anything: her face was doing the talking, just as Toby's had for over a year.

'The thing is, Toby,' Henry started; he took a moment, and Sam knew he was struggling to find the right words, 'I was worried that me spending time with Sam would make you sad.'

'Why?' Toby said, as all small children do.

'Because you miss Mummy.'

Toby looked at Jean as if he was hoping for some sort of explanation. Jean smiled at him. This was a conversation that Henry needed to have with his son.

'Well, you see, I think I love Sam.'

Sam had to put a hand over her mouth to smother the sob that was trying to find its way out.

'I love Sam too,' Toby said, and he looked as if he thought all adults were mystifying.

'But I still love Mummy,' Henry said.

'Me too,' Toby said, in a voice that suggested he had no idea why his dad was stating the obvious.

'I was worried that if you knew that I loved Sam, you might think that I had forgotten about Mummy.'

Toby tilted his head to one side.

'Why?' There was that question again.

Henry smiled. 'You've been so sad for so long, Toby, and I didn't want to make it any worse.'

'But Sam is your friend and she makes you happy, like Juno makes me happy.'

'He does do that,' Henry agreed, reaching down to fuss Juno who had collapsed at Toby's feet.

'Why wouldn't Mummy want you to be happy?'

For a moment, Henry looked as if he couldn't quite believe what he was hearing.

'I don't know, buddy. It's complicated,

loving someone new after you've lost someone else.'

'We haven't lost Mummy. She's here,' Toby said, and pointed to his heart. 'She told me that before she left for heaven.'

Henry tried to smile, but his face crumpled with the emotion, and soon he was sobbing. This time, it was the little boy who threw his arms around his daddy.

'It's okay to be sad sometimes,' Toby said softly. 'I feel sad sometimes, but Juno always makes me feel better.'

Toby released his dad.

'Can I have some cake?' he asked Jean, and everybody laughed.

'I think that is an excellent idea, Toby.' Jean nodded. 'And then maybe you and Juno can show me some of the new tricks you've learnt.'

After the cake had been eaten, Toby, Juno and Jean went off through the gate to the orchard, and Sam and Henry were alone. Henry stood up and walked over to Sam, holding out his hand.

When she took it, he pulled her to her feet and led her back to the swing seat.

'I have underestimated my son again,' Henry said, before opening his arms to Sam. Without a moment's hesitation, she folded herself into his embrace.

'He is wise beyond his years.'

'He reminds me of his mum,' Henry said, and Sam could feel him tense beneath her. 'Sorry,' he added.

Sam moved so that she could see Henry's face. 'Don't be. You don't ever have to worry about talking about Beth,' she reassured him, saying Henry's wife's name for the first time.

'I can't promise it won't be without its challenges, Sam. I loved my wife, and I still miss her every day . . . but I know that I love you, and I can't bear to be apart from you. I also want you to know that I heard what you said, and if this isn't what you want, then . . . then just tell me.'

Sam held up a hand to cradle Henry's face.

'Of course it's what I want. I said

what I did because I thought it would be easier for you to walk away.'

'I didn't want to.'

'I know. You love your son, and that's one of the many things I love about you.'

'You love me?' he asked softly.

Sam chuckled, and then reached up and kissed him. Henry returned the kiss, and before Sam knew it she was being held tightly in his arms.

'I love you,' she said, a little breathlessly, when they finally broke apart. 'And I love your son.'

'I love you too.' Henry kissed her again. 'And I'm pretty sure Toby has already given you his seal of approval.'

Sam turned her head. Jean and Toby were standing on the other side of the fence, both of them smiling. Juno and Georgie appeared and started to bark.

'Apparently, everyone is in favour,' Sam said. Henry pulled her close to him again, and she knew that she never wanted him to let go.

25

'Go easy, bud,' Henry said, before bending down and kissing Sam on the head. 'We don't want another broken window.'

'Sorry, Dad!' Toby shouted. Toby had grown so much that he was almost up to his dad's shoulders. Juno barked as he waited for Toby to kick the football back in his direction. Georgie was acting as goalkeeper, but as soon as Toby kicked the ball, Georgie was right in there racing Juno for it.

Sam laughed.

'Who would have thought you would have had a garden full of dogs?' she said as she looked to the rest of her pack, who were lolling around having worn themselves out playing football.

'Who would have thought, Mrs Wakefield?' Henry said, reaching over for her hand and kissing it. 'What can I say? You have had an amazing influence on my life.' Then he leaned forward and ran his hand gently across her growing belly. Sam placed a hand over his, and for a moment they waited. Their new baby was quick to make his or her presence felt.

'Who would have thought I would have found you?' He kissed her.

'Not me,' Sam said. They had been married for nearly two years now, and she still couldn't quite believe it. 'But I do keep telling you that dogs have magical powers.' They both smiled as they watched Toby charging around with the two dogs.

'As do you,' Henry said, and Sam rolled her eyes.

'Hardly.'

'You saved my son, and you saved me.' His eyes were serious, and so Sam lifted a hand to smooth away the slight frown.

'I never thought I would be able to trust someone enough to marry,' Sam said. 'You saved me too, and now look at me.' She cradled her stomach.

'Well, let's agree that we each saved each other.' Henry moved his face close to Sam's, and they locked eyes for a second before he leaned in for another kiss.

'Dad, stop kissing Sam, and come and play football!' Toby shouted, but with a wide smile on his face. 'Sam, can you be referee? You know how Dad cheats.'

'I do not!' Henry said indignantly as he ran up to his son and snatched the ball off him.

'Penalty to Toby!' Sam called, watching as Henry shook his head in disbelief and Toby grinned at her.

Sam settled back in her chair to watch her family — human and canine — play the scruffiest game of football she would ever see.

'Don't forget to take your vitamins,' Jean said, taking the seat beside her and placing the box on the table.

'As if you'd let me forget.'

'Never,' Jean said, smiling at her.

Sam picked up the box and dutifully took the pill as she had been told, all the while taking in her family, old and new. The one thing in life she'd thought she would never have. She could feel Jean's eyes on her, and she turned and smiled. Jean smiled back with that look. The one that told Sam Jean had known this was going to happen all along.

We do hope that you have enjoyed reading this large print book.

Did you know that all of our titles are available for purchase?

We publish a wide range of high quality large print books including:
Romances, Mysteries, Classics
General Fiction
Non Fiction and Westerns

Special interest titles available in large print are:
The Little Oxford Dictionary
Music Book, Song Book
Hymn Book, Service Book

Also available from us courtesy of Oxford University Press:
Young Readers' Dictionary
(large print edition)
Young Readers' Thesaurus
(large print edition)

For further information or a free brochure, please contact us at:
Ulverscroft Large Print Books Ltd.,
The Green, Bradgate Road, Anstey,
Leicester, LE7 7FU, England.
Tel: (00 44) **0116 236 4325**
Fax: (00 44) **0116 234 0205**

LONG DISTANCE LOVE

AnneMarie Brear

Fleur Stanthorpe, an Australian, arrives in Whitby to live out a dream after surviving cancer: opening a book-shop café before returning home after the summer. Only, she hasn't counted on meeting gorgeous Irishman Patrick Donnelly. He is looking for a solid relationship for the first time since his divorce five years ago — but she is having her last fling at freedom before going back to family and re-sponsibilities. What will happen when the summer draws to an end and it's time for Fleur to leave?